More Praise for

Silence the Bird, Silence the Keeper

"Like a stone from a slingshot, a bird on the wing, Christopher David Rosales's elegant, lyric, dynamic tale of perseverance and dignity in a brown, near-future Los Angeles soars from the lower depths and pierces the Cyclops-eye of América's well-armed political and economic elites as it seeks its goal in light."

— Michael Mejia, author of *Forgetfulness* and NEA Fellow

"This novel reaches into the back of your mind, the base of your skull, and it urges forth memories and feelings and images you didn't know you had, but that now you'll never forget."

— Stephen Graham Jones, author of *Ledfeather* and NEA Fellow

"This novel treats revolution, love, betrayal and magic with equal adeptness and intelligence. In a world that is at once ours and foreign Rosales makes characters that will be remembered when the novel is done. This is a truly fine piece of work."

— Percival Everett, author of *Erasure* and winner of the
Guggenheim Fellowship for Creative Arts

Published by Mixer Publishing
Chicago, Illinois

www. mixerpublishing.com

Cover & Interior Design: Weiyi Kong
Author Photo: J. Michael Martinez

Published in the United States of America

978-0-692-47190-6

Silence the Bird, Silence the Keeper

a novel by

Christopher David Rosales

mixer publishing

What you have heard is true. He swept the ears to the floor with his arm and held the last of his wine in the air. Something for your poetry, no? he said. Some of the ears on the floor caught this scrap of his voice. Some of the ears on the floor were pressed to the ground.

Carolyn Forché, "The Colonel"

One

In the city square where all our barrios met, even quiet steps frightened the swarms of dirty birds—up like ghosts, their wings swiped breaths off your face—and it was there we always whispered round the story about the baby. Not about the baby, but the baby's death. Murder, really.

See, the father and mother had been rocky since a while back. 1999, maybe, when the father—the Filero, we call him—joined up with the guerillas. The mother had fallen in love with him when he was still the owner of a bookshop, who would come home with books for her to read and make her sound out properly the words she didn't know. Sometimes, to tease him, and other times just because she liked a certain sound, she said the words wrong anyway. The Filero was a Californio with jagged scars up and down his arms, and said he always would be. She was just a poor poor puta.

So eventually, like many poor women, she fell in love with a rich man—a mafioso. The kind of guy who wears white suits and flies his helicopter everywhere, floats above the bombings and carjackings and kidnappings of Old L.A. County. Floats high above the Angelinos and their five-dollar bullets to the brain. The Mafioso touched down in her town with a politico, and offered the men jobs if they voted the right way. The men took them, the jobs running drugs barefooted across the chunky asphalt roads and the dusty ones between. Not the

Filero. He refused the extra money, instead working extra hours at the bookshop, funding his revolution with honest work.

The Mafioso came to visit when the men were on work—sometimes he visited the other wives. Mostly just the Puta, though she wasn't called that then. She was a caring woman. She would comb her black hair over one side of her head with one hand, shush the Mafioso's sweating upper lip with the other, and go and put her nipple in the baby's mouth. For that kind of cariña, the Mafioso was willing to wait.

But one day the Filero came home early from a mission. He'd blown up the parking structure beneath the bank tower off the freeway. He was tired. He'd spent all day running. He set his oiled machine gun on the table and his soiled bandalero over the chair, and needless to say he was hungry.

She was breastfeeding the baby, buck naked and sweating, and the Filero couldn't even blink, that's how tired he was. He thumbed through a manuscript of poems, hand-written, that one of the guerilla's hoped he would carry down at the bookshop. The Filero didn't like poetry. Especially the political poetry that so many young men were reading in his shop Friday nights, filling the cramped building with a fog of words and weed smoke. Mensaje de plata, he thought, Poema de mierda. Silver message, shitty poem. When the words went foggy on the manuscript in his hands, he tried, once, to blink, but his eyes latched closed.

How many moments passed in the dark, he wasn't sure.

The noise from the bedroom snapped his eyes open.

No sooner and his blade snapped open too.

The Puta screamed and the husband yelled "Puta" and we call her that always because of how things ended.

The Filero found the Mafioso climbing out the window, and he cut a big red gash in the ass of those white pants. That was all, and it seemed as close as anyone would ever get to touching the untouchables. Chut-chut-chut went the helicopter.

That wasn't the end of the story. The Mafioso was jealous, and one day he came back to our barrio, and this time he brought men with him, eyes bloodshot from the cocaine, and gazes slid around the small hut looking for the husband. The Filero wasn't home. He was out with the guerillas hiding in El Dorado Park off the 605 freeway running from our barrio of Clearwater to Playas. They'd just robbed another bank. The Filero wouldn't be back until dinner, but the Puta didn't tell the Mafioso that. Now she saw her infidelity for what it was: a desire to be better than this neighborhood. She saw her husband for what he was: just that. She told the Mafioso her husband was dead, and kept her eyes on the baby in her arms.

The Mafioso, still wounded, limped his fine white shoes across the swept dirt floor of the hut to the Puta, careful not to kick up dust. He had a hand wrapped around back to grip his right ass cheek. Behind him, the Puta saw, one of the men grinned at the Mafioso's plight, and raised a hand to cover his broad mustachioed mouth.

"He resembles the father." The Mafioso spoke in a clean, crisp, American accent, anger tumbling his voice too deep, maybe, for his own throat.

She'd been holding the baby at her breast since they came in, and her arms stayed that way—cradling—even after the Mafioso yanked the baby by one foot, flung it down headfirst, like the old men know to snap a snake.

The baby didn't even cry. There was very little blood—a dark pearl like a premature and improper earring called eyes to the tiny spiral of the ear.

When the Puta finally looked up from her baby lying tangled on the swept earth floor, the Mafioso and his white suit and white men were gone.

And when the Filero found out, he did a very foolish thing. He went to the police. He knew he'd never find the Mafioso and the police would never help, but he was grieving, no? So he went. Se fue. Like that he was already gone.

With his dead baby in his arms and his blade in his back pocket, the Filero waded through the birds and the people in the square. No one in the busy office building noticed that the baby was dead, not just sleeping; though the blanched face of the baby was the same color as the webbed scars on the Filero's forearms.

He spoke his story about the Mafioso to the police, who told him tell it to the chief, who said that mafiosos were the mayor's business. The Filero wasn't surprised. With downtown L.A. run by corporate interests, and the coastlines run by resorts, the middle grounds of the Clearwater barrios were open territories many had already abandoned to whoever would claim them their own. The jungles, as they were called, were not jungles at all. They had once been Watts and Compton, North Long Beach, Whittier, Paramount and Pico. The worst off had become wildlands no one lived in, that we knew of. The best off? The Filero had only to look at the floor his muddy boots stood on.

The Mayor opened the office door wide. He even acknowledged the Filero as if to say come in, and then he went and sat at the desk where he resumed writing, and without looking up said, "Go home."

The Filero studied the door—opened politely for him only moments before—and shook his head. In defiance or confusion, even he couldn't say.

Then, with new resolve, the Filero crossed the quiet carpet and lay the baby on the Mayor's desk. The blanket fell away to reveal the silence, the pale skin, and the soft spot on one side that was now a small blue bowl.

The Mayor looked away from the baby, removed his glasses and set them aside.

He asked the Filero's name and the Filero gave it: Rudy Sellers. The Mayor asked the baby's and the Filero said, "Fuck you." So the Mayor wheeled his chair back, spun around, and opened a filing cabinet.

"You live in the barrio off the ninety-one, yeah?" When the Mayor toed the chair around he had his head angled back to read the tiny print on the paper in his hands. He patted his chest pocket for the glasses that he then recognized were already open on the desk. He almost looked at the baby, but retreated. "What's the name on that nameplate right there?" When the Filero looked puzzled the Mayor said, "There," limply pointed, "right there on my desk."

Careful not to look at the baby on the desk, fearing he'd lose himself, the Filero welcomed the opportunity to read the large letters of the nameplate aloud. "Sam Marquesi."

"It says here you voted for Fitzgerald last election."

"At least I voted."

The Mayor smiled at that. "Well, maybe if Fitzgerald were here he would help you." The Mayor sighed. "But he's not." He folded in the arms of the glasses where they lay on the desk, looking as much for something to do with his hands as for some way to avoid discussing the baby. "You own that shop on Cherry Avenue, don't you? The one with all the lesser-known books." His lazy speech was an act, and it had begun to tax his own patience as much as the Filero's. His breathing picked up, his speech quickened. "I like those books—I like the poetry—you?"

"Not even a little."

The Mayor flushed red. For the Mayor, this answer seemed more obstinate than it was; the Filero was an honest man. "Then why carry it?"

"Kids need poetry."

"Adults don't need poetry?" The Mayor leaned forward, pleased with the new direction he'd taken the conversation.

Rudy knocked the desk with a knuckle. "I know what you're doing."

"The kids? They're old enough to write slogans for posters, eh? Posters they make in your shop where they meet to plan protests." Each time he made a new point, he touched the bridge of his nose like he missed his glasses there.

"Basta," Rudy said, leaning heavy on a fist on the desk. "Either things happen in a man's backyard that he can't control, or you're the one responsible for this thing that happened in yours." The Filero was pointing at the baby lit sickly by the daylight through the bird-shit on the window. "Admit to one. Well?"

Neither man would be the first to look. Outside, the square had filled with yellow sunlight, cracks in the earth and buildings and the lines in people's faces deepened. Birds pecked at the earth, at whatever squirmed there. Rudy must have known: if he didn't look at his baby, no one would.

The Mayor's stare journeyed across the desk—the two pens teeter-tottering, the stack of papers and what lay on top of them—and the Mayor reached slowly, tenderly, his fingers hovering nearer the blanket that had fallen away, the baby's bruised head either radiating cold or the room cold and the Filero just now noticing. The Mayor scissored open two fingers, and it seemed he wanted to take up the blanket's corner and cover the baby for the Filero.

The Filero's brow was a tight knot he thought he would have to cut to loose, but somehow the Mayor's manicured fingers, nearing his baby's blanket, they were slim and capable and Rudy felt they might untie him.

In the end, though, the Mayor only took his glasses up off the desk like he wanted them kept clean and, that close to the baby, they wouldn't be.

The Mayor's eyes set on the Filero to show that, after all, the Filero was in this alone.

So the Filero urged himself to look and, when he did, the Mayor stood. The Mayor took the Filero's forming tears as further accusations. The worst kind. After all, no man could stand to see another man cry.

"Their posters called my birds worse than rats in the plague." The Mayor bit a bottom lip to keep from shouting. All of this was more insulting than words. It hurt more. Hurt somewhere he couldn't place but he thought was his gut. "People come from all around to feed my birds," the mayor roared. "There are grandparents, and, and little children—when the birds all land," he slammed his fist on the desk, "it's like clouds. People will remember that. They won't remember you. They'll remember me and my birds. They won't remember that…" With the glasses, he pointed at the baby lying atop the desk, "They won't remember that paper weight."

The men studied each other's eyes.

They both remembered, no, realized, why the Filero had come.

The Mayor's hands shook when he put on his glasses, as if despite the growing fear he felt the need to see it all come into crisp focus. The Filero: the jagged scars on the slow steady arm, the fingering of the knife from the pocket and then, at the hip, the quick snap—the knife opens when the Filero crosses the carpet. Not to the Mayor. No, to the door. And just as dutifully as the Mayor had opened the door for the Filero, the Filero closes it, even uses the knob.

The soldiers found the Filero straddling the desk with the Mayor's tie knotted in his fist, stabbing and stabbing all the places that were most deadly. The baby's body still lay on a pile of disheveled paperwork off to one side of the desk, and the father had been careful not to disturb it.

That wasn't the Puta's only child. She'd got pregnant during her brief affair with the Mafioso and gave birth only eight months after her husband had been thrown in jail for murder and conspiracy— though there'd been no conspiracy at all and he'd readily admitted to the crime—and only eight months after her first baby had been buried someplace she never could find. She cried all through the pregnancy.

When she went to visit the Filero who, we were surprised, had forgiven her, she cried so much in the visitor's cell that he asked to have her sent away. In his cell he awaited the letters she dropped for him. When he got them they were always brittle in the places where the ink had run with her tears.

She brought the Mafioso's baby to the visitation cell and the Filero accepted the baby as his own, knowing full well that it wasn't. But then she cried with her head in his lap, drying her wet eyes and mouth there. She left black and red makeup streaks all down the crotch of his only clothes for the week, and he'd not get to wash them, and he knew he'd be teased and maybe beaten. In fact, as he rumbled off leaving whatever he could as debris—her letters, the picnic she'd packed, the baby's spit rag—the guard was already chuckling and calling the Filero all the words he knew for a woman's parts. The guard knew a lot.

The Puta heard him calling them out long after her husband had gone, and even as she gathered the things left scattered round, and even later in her hut while she prepared the baby for bed.

Rudy Two, she whispered.

The Filero finally died one night, in a prison fight, because he'd said we should send our stories to whoever would print them—that is, if we didn't have the balls to print them ourselves. The man with whom he'd shared his cell was a long lean poet with far-reaching arms, and he believed strongly that the only place for our poetry was with our people. For once, the Filero struck less than got struck.

The long poet watched the Filero bleed out in the corner, and had died in his own bed by the time the guard slid in his breakfast tray.

So we just called the baby Rudy, because it was down to one.

The Puta, she continued to hear all the words for a woman's parts echo like they were inside of her. Like they were her. She blamed herself for things getting as bad as they had, and she began to cry with her face against the baby's belly and she used her brown hair as a towel on his chest.

Her mother's ghost stood in the doorway of the hut, skin and bone and glasses swinging from a chain around her neck. "For christ's sake, you're going to drown him."

We all believe that the Puta would have. She hurt. Even putas have feelings. That's what some of us would say. The old ones wouldn't say that, of course, because they didn't talk that way. They'd just cough, take their seats on the soiled benches in the square, and go on feeding the endless birds. You know, you could pinch the stale bread into a hundred pieces the size of a bullet, and still you'd never get to every one.

Two

It was hard to say how Rudy Two's son, the one called Tre, thought back then.

He stood in the square, against the town hall's muraled wall, smoking from a joint pinched tight between his fingers. He was young, maybe eighteen, but more than that he was mean and we didn't want to admit he might think like us—even if he did.

He had one foot kicked back flat against the painted wall, and grease smudged the toe of his shoe where it wore thin from all the gear-shifting in traffic. The motorbike wasn't far. Wasn't ever far. He'd left it in the shade in an alley so its red wouldn't draw more attention. Still, it was getting late. The sun in the square was orange now. The birds were returning, one by one like fat drops of oil splashing at his feet. They hobbled near the broken fountain, where the old men fed them bread.

Another young man called Junior lumbered across the cobbles carrying a crushed envelope. Junior, big and babyfaced but no younger than Tre, almost leaned on the mural to catch his breath but dropped that hand with the other to both knees and went on panting. Tre went on leaning coolly, thinking cool thoughts and staring at the broken fountain in the center of the square. At least three different statues of three different mayors had stood there in his lifetime. He smirked at the crumbled concrete loafer, all that remained of one. These politicos, and their reverse Cinderella dreams. He imagined the same old loafer passed along from statue to statue, from mayor to mayor, from prince to prince. His sister, Nora, was back home, pining for her own kind of slipper offered by some wealthy politico or decorated militant. Tre coughed a laugh to himself. No one in his family knew how to live in this world without depending on others. No one knew how to survive. No one but him.

The painted figure in the mural that towered above the young men was sleek, rosy, and stiff, with a blank expression that could have been mistaken for … Tre theorized constipation, but it was probably meant to show purpose. He offered Junior the joint, but Junior waved it away, still catching his breath.

Tre smoked deep. "Too good, or what?"

"We're self-employed." Junior clutched his heaving side. "A business man's got to set some standards."

"Oh, and you think this is that kind of business?" Tre laughed. The best way to survive was to adopt new standards, moral and otherwise. At first, his new standards had been a tight heat in the muscles of the jaw and behind the eyelids. At first they were a new skin tight on his face like steam. At first. He checked his cheap plastic watch and held the other hand out for the letter. "Come on."

"You come on." Junior finally caught his breath, but didn't relax. "And don't lean against that mural, Mamón." Junior handed the envelope over.

"Why not?" Tre angled his head back until the mural sprawled upside down from his forehead, pouring into the blue. "Who is this guy, anyway?"

"It's the fucking mayor," Junior said. "Don't play dumb."

"Huh." Tre may have been reading the letter. He looked at it, at least. Then he used it to tap the mural over his shoulder. "I thought it was Ricky Ricardo." Yes, his new standards eliminated the guilt, because it was impossible to feel guilty for taking a life he resented.

"Ricky who?" But Junior squinted one eye up and down, nodding slow recognition at the mural now.

Tre crushed the papers into a ball and tossed them at his feet. He was already laughing at Junior. The joint, Tre plucked from his lips and rubbed out on the manhole sized bottom button of the mayor's coat. "The money?"

"Un uh." Junior said. "After."

Tre shrugged, held his hand out again. Junior let a handful of bronze bullets fall one by one into Tre's greasy palm. Tre smiled then. Some things he could still feel the old way. Bullets cold as ice chips in his sweaty palm. A girl's pussy, hot as a washcloth. He was easy to please.

"Do you ever…" Junior swallowed.

"Do I ever what?"

"Do you ever feel guilty?"

Without opening his mouth Tre licked the outsides of all of his teeth. He shook his head no.

Yeah. It was easier for us to pretend he didn't think like us. Maybe that he didn't think at all. Still.

A single bullet fell from Tre's palm, turning round, and bounced once on the cobbles.

Junior groaned and bent to pick up the ringing bullet but, before he could reach, Tre toed the shiny thing like a snuffed cigarette.

"Not that one," Tre said.

Junior smacked his lips. "That shit cost me five dollars. What you talking about, not that one?"

"You've got yours. I've got mine. Standards, homie," Tre said, grinning. "Standards."

Three

Rudy had been waiting twenty minutes for a student in his office, twenty minutes now spent sighing over a book on violentology and trying to lift the baggy drapes of his eyelids long enough to see the clock and was it time to go.

Though Rudy heard his own story from us, growing up, and even though we teased him at the ocean that, because of his mother's tears, he had become immune to drowning, he never insulted or even kidded us back. He was rough on the playground and worked hard at the books, but as he got older, he was fifty-six now, he got softer—instead of the other way around. His face took on the shape of someone in mourning. His eyes were always dark and his brow deeply wrinkled, and though we said to each other the deep lines down the sides of his mouth had been worn into his face in the womb by his mother's tears, really they were there because he had to work so hard to smile. He was a professor now at the local university and he was well known for speaking out against inhumanity, corrupt politics, and the impunity of criminals and the government both. Which is to say he was not very well known at all, or well thought of except by a few acquaintances and academics.

Tut, who was not much of an academic but much more than an acquaintance, leaned his bald head in the doorway, raised his eyebrows at the time on the clock, and sighed. "Don't wait on them, buddy. These snobby students of ours wouldn't wait on your class if there were a ball to get to. Whatever Leticia made for dinner will get cold."

"She's a beautiful woman, Tut, but a boring cook. She doesn't like to aggravate my stomach."

"That's why when I make you my special chili, the secret recipe isn't onion powder, it's crushed antacid. You let your work stress you too much. Go home. Happy guts cure everything."

Rudy smiled and waved goodbye. "Happy guts do." And anxious ones?

On the desk: a pen propped in a brass cylinder that he'd received when he made Chair of the English department, a black and white photo of La Playa Pier's amusement area before the naval base was built, and a framed photo of his family. He swept all this into a deep locking drawer. He gathered up his coat, his jacket, his sweater and his notebooks, flipped the light switch and locked the door behind him.

The student, a chubby girl with expensive earrings, didn't rush across the wide parking lot to his distant designated parking space. Rudy's bearing never impressed upon anyone that sort of urgency. Perhaps the only impression he made was that of a rubber stamp recently used—he left so much of himself in his writings that his presence was a ghostly indecipherable shape. He had a key raised up in the air and was squinting through his bifocals to study it, huddled inside all his layers against the cool ocean breeze. The Volvo added the smell of burned oil to that breeze even when it wasn't running. He shook his head and studied yet another key.

"Dr. Sellers." The student's heels clacked closer. "I don't understand."

"I had it marked," he said. "I swear I marked it with the—there we go."

She slid between him and the door. "Dr. Sellers?"

He pushed his glasses higher up his nose. High enough, and there was a ridge off of which nothing perched could fall. But he didn't like to draw attention to it. He was just like his father the Mafioso, who he didn't know from anything but reputation and who'd been vain enough to wear pants in rich men's pools, even his own, to hide the scar snaking down the back of his thigh; the scar that the Filero, Rudy One, had given him.

Rudy sighed, "...but you didn't check your sources. Your paper's full of errors. Half the works you cite are nothing but pure—well, they're propaganda."

"According to you."

Rudy used an arm like a waiter to gesture rather than escort her away from his car. "I guess we disagree."

She stomped away and he took the opportunity to get in the car and close the door, but he could see in the side-view mirror that she hadn't left yet. She dropped a finger to her thigh, tapped it a few times. She mouthed something that he couldn't hear through the window. He rolled it down.

"What was that?" he asked, but she shook her head lightly, as if to say no thanks. His heart got the better of him, as it always did in confrontations with students, especially the young women that made him think of his daughter, Nora. He sighed. "You can write it over, if you want. For half credit."

She pursed her glossy lips at him, and this time she did say, "No thanks. It's just propaganda, anyway." Like she had a better idea, she said, "At least, according to you."

The car lugged up the onramp, shaking around Rudy. The riverbed snaked into sight below. The ocean rolled away behind him, and on all sides palm trees flagged the ghettos—he felt good. He'd stood up to that student.

But his smile reminded him that she'd smiled, and that she must have had a reason for it. He didn't think he'd done anything wrong but that didn't mean she couldn't report him. Damn. He hated this feeling of always being the guerillas' little sister and the government's child, and something about his face, the drag of his brows, his eyelids, his jowls and the sides of his lips: despite his pride the smile just made him look mournful.

Everyone knew that smile. Some of us said it was the Puta's grief, that it had taken his whole life to sink through the callous skin he'd inherited from his father the Mafioso, but now that it had he couldn't wring it from his heart no matter how he tried. Some of us said it was his own grief. Not for his past, but for the future. That his smarts were a burden. Because he knew all along what would happen to you if you kept living in a place like this one had become, and yet all he had was smarts. He hadn't the ganas to try to leave. He'd studied the past. Studied the globe. Studied the birds to distract himself when it all became too much. Still he smiled his smile, slapping the wheel to the smooth jazz he liked to listen to on his way from the shining towers of the university to the ramshackle houses of his own neighborhood, a neighborhood normal people like us could afford.

Four

They were a family of four: Rudy, his wife Leticia, their son Rudy Three who went by Tre, and their seventeen-year-old daughter Nora who was their prized possession. They used to have dinner together but this night was like most since the kids had become teenagers. Tre patted his father on the back, kissed his mother on the forehead, and left with his backpack and motorcycle helmet on one arm, mumbling something about a date through the hunk of bread still in his mouth. No sooner had Leticia wiped Tre's crumbs off her forehead than Nora swarmed into the kitchen wearing a dress half hidden beneath a topcoat, and left lipstick on Leticia's frowning forehead where the crumbs had been. Leticia dipped a napkin in a waterglass. Rudy groaned and removed his glasses and hooked a finger over the bridge of his nose. Both parents listened to the front door shut.

"She looked good," Leticia said, the wet napkin forgotten in a hand, the red kiss like a third eye.

Rudy pushed the same old cornmeal around with a spoon, writing in a fancy script, the letters fading.

"You wouldn't have to worry about it if we left."

"Where would we go? How?"

"Nevermind." She put her left hand on his.

He rubbed the tan line where her wedding ring had been before they'd pawned it. He looked up, smiled with his brows bunching, and took the wet napkin from her. He cradled her chin, and scrubbed her forehead. "You missed something."

Five

Tre leaned his bike into the turn and wound his way through the frozen traffic. We always said he leaned into everything that way. He didn't ever seem to be trying too hard at anything at all.

He flipped up the visor of his helmet and checked his watch. Tapped it once or twice. "Piece of shit." When he flipped the visor down the sunset shimmered pink across it.

Slowing each time he passed a luxury sedan, he'd crane his neck to see the plates. He stopped behind a long brown car with dark windows, checked the license number scribbled on the back of his hand against the license plate on the sedan. The scribbles across his hand had smeared with sweat, but they were clear enough to see they didn't match. He rode on, calling different curses for each different rich man's car he passed. Passat equaled pussy. Fiat equaled faggot. Benz equaled bends over and takes it in the ass. He laughed, fogging his visor, and relished the blindness. When the fog retreated and revealed the crowded street, he closed his eyes—his right elbow clipped hard against a side-view mirror but he kept them closed. Since his parents had begun to pawn the family keepsakes he'd felt invincibly dead. Like the elimination of personal property was a slow and steady lowering of the coffin of their hope.

A horn honked twice and his eyes opened wide on a jeep changing lanes right in front of him. He swerved around it, barely, and a woman inside shouted, "You're going to kill someone."

"I hope so." He shouted spit onto his visor, and flipped her off.

The traffic was heavy in the intersection, and everyone was honking but no one going anywhere. Thankfully, this included his target in the brown sedan. Using the balls of his feet, Tre stepped his bike up alongside the rear door, took the .38 from his waistband, and shot three times through the closed backseat passenger window.

Inside the white starburst of glass a bloody head slumped out of sight.

The driver kicked his door open and peeked his head out. Tre cut a mock salute across his helmet. The driver left the door open when he ran, looking back only once, and casually. He slowed to a jog, and then a walk three cars down.

Tre set the kickstand, left the bike running. He opened up the rear door and ducked inside over the dead man. He felt around for wallets. A lot of these guys kept two, one just for these sorts of occasions and a real one … here, right along the warm inner thigh. Something shiny caught Tre's eye even through the dark visor. A wristwatch—Rolex—and he traded the man's watch for his. He took the time to put his broken watch on the man's wrist, laughing, and to adjust the thick-wristed man's watch to his own. Then he removed all the cash from the wallets, but not the cards, and put them back too. It was important that the hit not look like a robbery. Whoever had hired him wanted to send some kind of message. But, still, all dude needed now was a coin on each eye—he wouldn't miss the paper money.

Outside, the horns honked when he mounted the bike. No sirens yet. He heeled back the kickstand and lurched forward, then rolled, easing his way through the maze of metal. A few people inside the cars he passed ducked their heads. Most of them watched, heads tilted out their windows.

Tre lowered the kickstand, dropped the remaining cartridges into his pocket, took off his helmet, and tucked it with the pistol into his backpack. Then he made sure he'd brought the right romance flick. On the cover, a man and woman faced each other across a wide night sky, and a carrier pigeon hovered between them, pinching in its beak a bannered note reading the title.

He zipped up his backpack and went to the door of the girl's house. There was no one around. And besides that, none of the streetlamps worked so no one could see him anyway. He checked the Rolex, pressed it to his ear and listened. He couldn't hear the watch's delicate turnings over the sounds of the naked-bellied children playing like faint shadows in the street, the neighborhood dogs whining from a safe distance for him to feed them, or the music on the radios inside all the windowless houses.

From the porch, he stared at his red motorbike parked alone in what was left of the street mostly dirt now. The occasional tuft of grass or chunk of asphalt. The bike looked strong on roads like this. Rode over them with ease, after the mods: the stolen tires, the halogen bulbs. Sure it was used up. Scratched. Frankensteined out of junkyard parts and spray-painted bright red to hide the bolts and stitches. Sure it had seen better days. Still, around here, Tre was somebody because of that thing.

She opened the door, wearing a peasant style blouse that made a wing of the arm blocking his entrance. Her pink tongue licked her lips, not horny but hungry. "You're late."

"So long as your period ain't."

"That might be how you talked to hoodrats before but that ain't how you talk to me."

"Okay, okay." He kissed her dark cheek, unzipping the bag as he did so, and then tugged out the VHS tape. He'd got it out of someone's house just this week. They'd had DVDs but no one he knew had a player, and he hadn't had room on his bike for something that big. "I brought popcorn, too."

She smiled, showing white teeth; rare, anymore. Kissed him again.

He licked his lips. She was wearing that peppermint lip gloss he'd gotten her.

"Where'd you get the money for popcorn?" she asked.

"I got a job." He knew she wanted to ask him for more details but would stop herself. Girls had to, around here. Love didn't require good men and good women; just men, and just women. "Are you going to let me in, or what?"

"Where'd you get the money, I said."

So this one was different.

"Give me a chance to explain?"

Six

Nora on her way to the dance. Always on her way to somewhere. That's just how we knew her. A little girl never satisfied to sit still, grown up into a young woman never satisfied with her station. Slow hair falling, swinging, shining. Smiling, always smiling. Cheeks touched by the pink sun sliding into the water beyond the parade deck, her passive dissatisfaction had grown into active intent. That's just exactly how we knew her but she didn't know herself that way. Like most pretty things who are not raised beneath the magnifying glass eyes of dissatisfied parents—quite the opposite; she could do no wrong—the few things she knew as her flaws, she obsessed over. She saw herself as too tall, too slender, too whimsical when a young woman her age should be serious. She forced frowns, but her brow cramped. She fought smiles but they won. And she only felt at ease any more when she was working toward changing herself, her life in her parents' increasingly poor home, when she crossed the parade deck and saw herself through the young Capitan's hazel eyes. He held down the Pike, kept eyes on the port.

Many girls went there for this reason—the rich, the college girls—to silently taunt the soldiers with their hips and hair and things. To show off the clothes Mommy and Daddy had bought them. There was no need to pass through the parade deck to get to the ship where the dance was already starting, except, to the girls, all the soldiers and their stiffly starched clothes and their unflinching stares were good enough reason.

Sometimes, if the skirts were short enough, if the blouses partially buttoned or tied up above a crescent belly button, the soldiers would get shiftless, their eyes would lead their heads to turn their shoulders and all was lost. The Capitan would berate them. The girls laughing all the while.

But none of Nora's friends ever drew the Capitan's eyes. None of them saw how green they could be in the morning, how yellow they'd flash at night. Like a hunting cat, she liked to think walking across the parade deck, feeling light and flitty.

The families walked by the unit, armed and in formation near the Ferris wheel, like the soldiers were sentries made of stone, like they were commemorating the squelched "revolution" or "rebellion" or "terrorist attack" depending on who you asked. It was now just a memory as fragmented as the ocean's reflections of the Ferris wheel's lights. Not long ago, but already spinning into an oceanic depth of forgetfulness.

A little boy dropped his ice cream cone a few feet from a soldier's polished boot-toe and the mother picked the cone up hastily, stuck it in the child's hand upside down.

Most of the girls had walked ahead to the dance at the Queen Mary, and their parents had paid, and there'd be soldiers there who were allowed to flirt and talk and dance. Nora wasn't allowed at those things. Too political, her father said. Even if she were allowed she wouldn't get there til tomorrow, walking as slow as she did past the Capitan.

His collar was high and his back was straight and beside that she couldn't have said much about him. When all the other girls had passed, and she was the only one left, he raised his sword to his nose like he was cutting himself in two—he would be that way, too. Two men, one very stern and the other very playful.

He shouted a command: "Eyes, right."

The entire unit snapped their chins into line with their right shoulders, focusing on Nora.

She stumbled once. Again. She brushed her brown hair back of her ear and smiled.

The Capitan's eyes were lodged in the shadow of his cap's visor, like gems in a felt case, and she'd only seen those in commercials or on the rich girls' ears. He didn't smile back. He didn't even flinch. He stood there cut in half by that shiny sword, and only after she'd crossed the parade deck did he call for the ranks to shift like gears into stiff stances facing the city. A strange, sourceless, singing met her burning ears, reminding her of her blushing cheeks, and she moved on quickly.

When she got to the line for the Queen Mary her friends already stood at the front of the swaying wooden platform, showing their purses to the guards. The singing was louder now, and she looked back on the parade deck. A long procession of women wound down the street clutching signs and candles growing brighter as the pink night turned to grey. They sang in the street, and their mumbled prayers seemed a chorus with the sound of the water jostling the boats in the harbor. The signs they held said, Where's my brother, sister, mother, father, child? They said, Will we only find them once we are in heaven?

The young Capitan shouted a command and the soldiers filed off one by one, to form a line at the edge of the parade deck.

Behind Nora, a girl said, "I hope they don't ruin it." She patted her bell shaped hair. "So are you actually going in this time, chica, or did you just come to stare at your boyfriend again?"

Above and beyond the parade deck, downtown Playas couldn't shrug loose the haze. Somewhere past all that was Nora's home, her neighborhood, and since she wasn't allowed to attend the dance, and didn't have the money anyway, she'd be heading home sooner than later.

The girl offered Nora an extra set of fake diamond earrings inside a small felt case. Beneath the bell of her hair were two earrings of her own. "A uniform ain't enough." She looked down her nose at the other girls like a teacher. "Unless there's cash in its pockets."

All of them laughed. Even Nora, faking it. These girls always challenged her. She was two years younger, slightly less desperate, and had tested up into their class. So they both nurtured her and nagged about what they called, "Nora's Naiveté." She believed she didn't need to throw herself at any and every man that passed wearing a badge. She believed she need only, well, believe. Believe in one. And she'd seen him.

She'd seen her Capitan, and he'd seen her, and for Nora that was enough. Even better, he'd seen her not as herself but as someone of his own station. That was about much more than money. He'd seen her as she knew he could make her: what she always tried to be. It's just, she was getting tired of faking.

Nora shook her head at the earrings. "Take them," the girl ordered, furrowing her brows and lowering her voice like a military man. She raised her bladed hand as if expecting a returned salute.

"No." Nora stroked her lapels and her hair. She shook her head at the earrings. "I don't need them."

The other girl snapped the case shut.

Seven

Tre walked through the alley, looking up for oranges in the trees he passed. He came here often, lately. When he was sick he ate oranges, rind and all, like his mother had told him her mother had told her to do. He was sick now. Nausea with sour spice spidering his sinuses, and an ache flaring from the base of his spine in the shape of a rooster's claw. It wasn't nerves. It wasn't guilt. Damn, why had Junior asked him if he ever felt guilty? All that meant was that Junior did. It didn't say anything about Tre, did it? He came back up the main street, and to lighten his mood he chucked an orange at the children kicking stones in the dirt. They ran. When he got to the corner house, a car was parked near his motorcycle where the grass would have been had the yard grown any.

The shining window sank and ringed fingers scissored out an envelope.

Tre bit into an orange, chewed, took his time. It wasn't ripe, and the tartness tugged at the muscles in his jaw. He squinted into the dark car and said, "I thought it came through Junior. Not like this."

"This one's pressing." The voice was quiet, deliberate, and not secretive.

"There's a million of us, no?"

"Who said you're the only one I've seen?"

Still chewing, Tre took the envelope. The children down the street had frozen to watch, but when they saw him see them they shot into action. Laughed at nothing. Dribbled rocks foot to foot. Tre tossed the orange aside. When he held the note up to flip through what was inside, he smelled the zest on his fingers.

An old man in a cowboy hat, the one we call Viejo, happened to walk by with his walking stick in hand, and nodded to Tre and then to the car as if it were the live thing with the voice.

The ringed hand hanging out the window flicked a finger in a greeting and the Viejo walked on. The Viejo has said to us that he heard Tre ask, "How'd you know I'd be here?"

"I didn't," the voice said, "I was just passing through." The tinted window was already rising. "And there you were. Picking oranges."

Tre jutted his lower lip, nodded. Seemed to agree that all things, after all, were that simple. Or relent they could be.

Eight

The morning the nice car came for Rudy we were all in an uproar, sure it meant something bad. Maybe he'd finally pissed off the wrong people. The car nosed down the road slow as ships, swayed in to dock at the crumbled curb out front of their house. It was so quiet, so unexpected, it was like it had been there as long as the house, longer even, a big black block that we all inscribed with our own meanings, our own fears.

We peeked out our windows. We made excuses to walk past their home. No one exited the car. Someone joked that it was a mortician passing through the neighborhood who thought he might park and wait for business, but no one laughed.

Then we realized the nice car was there in honor of Rudy, to take him to speak at a conference at the convention center downtown. Rudy left the house wearing a pair of hands like goggles: Leticia's hands.

Nora was saying, "Don't peek, Daddy. Keep them closed." Her skirt twirled each time she beamed her smile from her father to the car.

Leticia dropped her hands into a hug around Rudy's waist. His own hand shot to cover his mouth. "Oh, my."

Despite Rudy's protests, his wife and daughter had concluded that the Volvo was too ugly for a keynote speaker, and we all watched him get into the fancy car with his daughter—she wanted to be just like him, we thought. His wife, Leticia, waved. She'd sent Tre word through the neighborhood to be here; words hopscotched across town by barefoot children more dependable than the postal service these days. Half as likely to steal from you. Skittish, overactive, efficient, cooing kid stuff to each other.

You could tell Leticia was disappointed that everyone was there to witness that good morning except her son Tre, by the way she watered the lawn with the hose as an excuse to look for him up one side of the block and down the other. In the flowerbed, their metal sprinkler sat crushing a honeysuckle.

Leticia watched the square, hot and lazy with sunlit dust, all the birds perched up in the rain gutters and under the eaves of windows, making the edges of the tall thin buildings look alive and breathing. Beyond that square, she could imagine Tre in some shack in one of the other barrios. In the arms of a woman. Probably that dark one. Oh, her boy. She'd always been able to call up images of him—her imagination, yes, but she knew him so well that she knew the images to be true. And so did he; she knew that too. Which was why he'd been spending more and more time away from home, ducking out the back window just as she walked in with a basket of laundry. Tre couldn't help it. He was such a raw energy he projected himself onto the white sheets of peoples' inquiring minds. She, we, everyone, thought he could have been a great man. But it was as if, knowing we'd strung the nice white sheet up in the backyard, and knowing we'd all been invited over to sit and to watch the great film of his life, he'd slipped like a bandit over the wall, knifed the sheet to shreds, and smashed the projector down on the hard black alleyway. Anyways, because it was in his nature to project his light, and because we'd been deprived of the greatness, all we saw was the bad shadow looming on the tatters. All except his mother.

Later we figured that if Tre hadn't slept over at his girl's house in the barrio none of this would have happened. Because he was used to a poor house, sure, but one with windows, and when he woke up under that Negra's arm, even after he lifted it, a weight remained on his chest. He woke her with coughing, mopping his sweating forehead with the back of a discarded drawing he'd done. The roosters crowed. The street dogs barked. Neighbors shouted. The day began in chaos, Tre said to us after. How else could a day like that end?

Leticia shook her head at the square, at the no one walking through it to come and make her feel better. Tre had missed a big thing here.

We were all real impressed with Rudy. Even the more catty gossips we didn't like from down the block had to admit that it was a nice car and Rudy looked pretty happy. For him, of course. A nice car, except there was rust on the chrome in places. But you couldn't even see it unless you looked real hard when it drove off. Then you could see it eating up the bottom of the bumper.

Children strutted in the streets, Leticia watching. The nice car backfired turning Rudy and Nora around the corner. At the sound like gunfire, the children flurried out in all directions, bare feet flapping dust into the lowest piece of sky.

Nine

In the back seat of the nice car, Rudy felt Nora try to wriggle the fingers of her hand clamped between his own. "I'm sorry," he said, and let her go.

"Nervous?" She shook out her hand and placed it on his knee.

He stared at her hand there, gone somehow from tiny to expansive the moment he saw it draped over the knob of his knee, which was bouncing up and down of its own accord. "Just the after effects."

The speech had come and gone without much incident. Within the tinted windows, they passed through everything like it were underwater, a blue mob of students and young people here just to listen. A few in the crowd had booed. Most had clapped. And here they were on their way back home. Rudy felt pressure like being underwater, too. Heard things from a long way off.

The driver said later that he had to smile because apart from the few words shared, father and daughter had cracked open books the moment they were seated in the car. Before and after the speech, they sat side by side in silence reading. Her: Of Love and Other Demons. He: Violentology and the future of U.S. Democracy.

When she didn't understand a word, she'd squeak in frustration, butterfly the book over a thigh, and wait until Rudy was done squint-

ing down his nose at the fine print of a note, at which point they
would each take the other's book, read with the tips of their tongues
corkscrewed out one side of their mouths, nod, hand the books back,
and relate to each other whatever they had read. Often they spoke at
the same time, and the driver had to puzzle through conversations
like: "Fifty murders a day the city lay submerged in its centuries long
torpor, but the assassination of journalists and professors, combined
with a mistrust of the educated elite on the part of the leftists, left no
doubt: he had been attacked by the same ash-colored dog with the
white blaze that had bitten Sierva María."

The driver said later he could not even distinguish their voices,
the father's rather high and soft for a man's, and, for a girl's, hers
rather low and husky.

Ten

This is the way it happened. The father and daughter conversed in the backseat, and the driver tuned up the radio to tune them out. Once they'd eased onto Pacific Coast Highway, Nora began to watch the ocean's waves, fringed with lacey white so near the port. She watched as if she might spot her Capitan out there, pining for her as she was for him. Rudy, oblivious beside her, tried to read his book but never turned a page, preoccupied as he was with his wife's desire to leave the country.

At the first red light a red motorbike appeared on Nora's side of the sedan. She glimpsed it, yeah. But when the light turned green, traffic trudged forward—the motorbike was lost somewhere behind them. She tried to get Rudy's attention but he didn't look up, suspecting it another question of semantics, and telling her instead that he would have to get her a bigger dictionary for her birthday.

She tapped his leg again.

He just said, "The biggest."

She pulled the book from his hands and his dry skin hissed over the pages.

Rudy raised his eyebrows high at her, as he was said to do to his students, and spoke with only his lower lip. "I'm all ears." This usually warranted an outburst of laughter because the process by which he raised his eyebrows and spoke through a tight jaw only served to stretch his face that much longer and increased his resemblance to a hound. But his daughter didn't laugh. At least, the driver didn't hear her laugh if she did. She leaned over her father and rolled down his window, but when she heard the driver warning, Don't do that, she leaned forward to ask him why.

The open window framed the assassin tugging a .38 from his waistband. Rudy was frozen, quizzical as always, maybe even taking a clear mental picture and inventory for some future essay on the relativism of violence in the wilds of civilization. Either way, he didn't say anything, and didn't tug Nora back down into her seat. Better this way, Rudy thought, alone. Tre would take care of them, the women. Rudy stared deep into the dark visor of the motorcycle helmet, and a blade of sunlight arced across it. The assassin took aim.

When the glare on the assassin's visor passed, he fumbled the .38, lost balance recovering it, and the bike swerved away. The bike reeled in, the assassin's knee sideswiped the door, and he knuckled the visor of the helmet up with a clack. The two men locked eyes, father and son. Now they knew.

Nora screamed. She'd seen the gun by then. After the fact, she never would admit to anyone Tre had been the assassin. A scandal like that could destroy them in the higher social circles. She always blamed it on some misunderstanding. No, better—our neighborhood gossip.

Traffic stopped suddenly and tossed father and daughter forward against the front seats. The driver's belly honked the horn. Outside, the bike whined against the downshift, tires screeched, and something tumbled across the street with the sound of body-punches.

By the time Rudy wrestled out of the car, Tre was already back on his bike trying to kick it down into first gear. The elbow of his jacket was worn through to his red skin, and blood seeped outward like ink in paper.

Rudy yelled, but Tre had already started the bike. He looked back only once, flipped his visor down, and sped off. The rear of the bike fishtailed every five feet or so and Rudy watched his son wriggle out of reach, bleeding, maybe seriously hurt, on that bike that could buck and dump him at any second.

Everyone who was there says the same thing.

Rudy picked the .38 up from behind a car's tire. He reached out with it, offering it to his son, or maybe hoping to use it as bait. It was like they say about parents who come upon their child after an accident, only to discover that the child's lost an arm. They pick it up. They put it back where it once was. They press it hard. Like things separated forever can be rejoined by love that easily. Either way, eventually Rudy put the .38 in his pocket, patted it through his wool slacks a few times, and mumbled after his son to be careful. To be careful and to come straight home.

Nora was out in the street by then, traffic trying to swell around them, and her telling the father he was crazy. She pulled her father back into the sedan, saying that hadn't been Tre. Tre was probably sleeping off a hangover somewhere. Never in a thousand years would Tre treat his bike like that.

They smiled stupidly for a while. Even the driver. He said the laughter wasn't so much at that joke about Tre and his bike, which they kept repeating. The laughter was all the fear that had tightened them up, all at once letting loose. The driver said their bellies felt filled with flung rubber bands.

After they'd left the coast and driven east on the freeway toward Clearwater, and the laughter had sunken into silence, Rudy put a cold hand between Nora's to be warmed up. The other hand, he pressed his face into, and he didn't make a sound the whole way home.

That's because he couldn't. Because his mother the Puta had cried and cried so much when he was in the womb that he would never be able to. We all knew that about him—about people. That grief is the only thing that doesn't train you for more of its own, that doesn't put more of itself inside you to grow. Grief only shrinks up the places you keep it. Drying up hearts and eyes like old fruits.

Eleven

Tre didn't show up at home that day, or the next, or the next. And neither father nor daughter told Leticia what had happened.

Leticia spent her time in the shade of the wide green avocado tree, swatting dust mats against its swayed trunk. With every swat she came up with a new reason they should leave Clearwater. Leave the country. But she'd say nothing of it until Tre returned. Above her, the green globes of the avocados shook.

While she was outside, Rudy took down a few books from the bookshelf in the corner of the living room, reached into his pocket, slid his son's .38 to the back of the shelf. He wanted to spare himself even one more discussion about leaving the country. Something he feared as much because it was a real option people were taking, as because he lacked the courage to acknowledge that all he'd written about this country was indeed true. He felt a strange suspicion that by writing of it he had caused it, too, and he lined the books up flush on the shelf.

Nora didn't think to say anything at all. She was going to a party the next day, at the Alamitos Ranch, hosted by a rich man who donated very much to the university, for posterity, and, for safety, to the Navy.

No, no one said anything. In fact, a breezy silence ran through the house, down its hall, into the bedroom where Nora tried on a dress before the mirror, and she had just begun to hum.

Twelve

At the university, the many palms lining its paths shrugged at the cloudy sky. In one of the dim classrooms, Rudy stood behind the podium lecturing a class of twenty freshmen, a remarkable half of which seemed somewhat interested. "Right," Rudy continued. "And what did Hambray say about that?"

They all roused up in their seats.

Rudy smiled at their sudden attention. "Oh. You all like your Hambray. Clarissa? No? Jonathan? Okay. Hambray said that conversation is the bridge we build between spirit and spirit. From the loudest shout," he shouted, which usually elicited a laugh but this time echoed in the silence, "to the most lowly whisper," he whispered. He turned to write on the chalkboard and saw the young Capitan standing all that time at the door.

The young Capitan walked in, flanked by two soldiers, and they all smelled of starch and sea salt.

Rudy looked over the class, over the nervous nail biters, over the tired faces waking now, and the indifferent smooth faces of the kids who never tried. One of these was the chubby girl who'd met him in the parking lot, and he rested his suspicion on her.

She glanced at the Capitan, who nodded some faint recognition. Rudy caught this briefest moment of conspiracy, sighed, and set the white nugget of chalk on the podium. He swiped his dusted fingertips around and around each other, watching the whorled fingerprints whiten.

"Mr. Sellers?" the Capitan asked. There was no malice in his voice. All of the students said later that the whole affair was pretty respectful. The dimmer ones even suspected their professor was being given some sort of honor.

"You've saved my reputation," Rudy said. "I was going to give them work over the break."

"Will you come with us, Sir?"

Rudy acknowledged the class with a smirk, as if it were all his own idea. He stumbled on his way to the desk, had to plant a hand firmly on its edge. Still, no one thought anything of it. He wasn't but fifty-six years old, if that, but to the students he could have been seventy. They said he'd stumbled due to eagerness or an old hip. Still, he must have known from his studies where they'd take him. "Just let me get my sweaters. The ocean air is chilly."

Thirteen

Nora's friend, Yesenia, the one who liked to sniff around the upper class parties, said she had been invited to this particular party because she was someone's cousin—Nora didn't know if it was true about being cousins, but she knew that at the very least Yesenia wanted to be somebody's wife. Yesenia was wearing her usual fake diamonds. She had encouraged Nora to do the same. Now, while they waited at the guard's shack at the bottom of a gentle hill, Yesenia swore under her breath that it was precisely Nora's lack of diamonds—fake ones, Nora reminded—that had them waiting in the custody of a pimpled soldier. The estate on the hill resounded with clinking glasses, stringed instruments, and laughter. The soldier showed his teeth to the girls, less a smile and more some display of his own physical worth.

"You're right," Nora said. "It's my fault your name wasn't on the list. Though," she pinched her naked earlobe, "I didn't claim mine would be."

Yesenia continued to mutter that the guard shack, small and hot as it was, made her feel like a dog. She fanned herself and flapped the bottom of her dress but despite the efforts to cool off succeeded only in widening the dark rings under her arms. Her hair had toppled more on one side than the other, but the other had toppled too.

The guard said later that Nora, unphased, almost stony except for the light sheen of sweat at her temples, stood with the best posture of anyone he'd seen. Navy, Army, Marines, anyone. She kept her long neck straight and her chin raised in such a way that he kept glancing off in whatever direction it pointed, half expecting to see something grand. All there was to see were the wasps hovering in the shaded white eaves of the guard shack. The compact room was bright to blinding, and there were no curtains on the glaring plastic windows.

Someone knocked on the open door and walked in.

Dressed in cream-colored slacks that draped his legs in shady pleats and folds, arms akimbo filling the doorway and the sun burning through his white shirt, was the Capitan from the parade deck. He caught Nora tracing his body's outline and let her eyes linger for a while before he cleared his throat.

When she raised her face to look at him that first time, he's since said, he wanted to turn around and seek out whatever it was deserved such a look.

"But my cousin—" Yesenia began.

The Capitan removed a blue handkerchief from his pocket and dabbed his forehead, his neck. He folded it over once and gripped each end, letting his arms hang in a cradle. He studied Yesenia down, then up. "Your cousin's not here," he said. "I hate to inconvenience you, but you should go."

Yesenia sputtered but he raised the handkerchief to his neck again and she took it wisely as some sign she should shut up.

Nora stood. She'd resigned herself to being poor, but more than that to feeling inconsequential, a thing she'd never truly believed of herself until now. She determined that, like any affliction, resignation was the only way this one could be lived with—but it did not rule out hope. Resignation was not hope's opposition the same way hate did not directly oppose love. Resignation had been a willingness to wait for the right time, the right man: this time, her Capitan. She smoothed her hands down the back of her dress.

The Capitan put his hand behind her back and, somehow pressing without touching her, eased her out of the stifling box into the cool ocean breeze of the Alamitos Ranch on the hill. How could it be that the time had come, and she had nothing to say to him and all he'd said to them was an order to leave? Yesenia followed them out, came to stand in front of them, tilting her head from side to side to aim her earrings at the sun, and for a moment the coolness retreated from the heat.

The Capitan turned and studied Nora's unpierced ears instead, instinctually raised a hand an inch to touch them before his back stiffened and he once again seemed that stern version of himself Nora knew from the parade deck.

"She'll be going now," he said, nodding to the guard, then Yesenia. Yesenia glared not at the Capitan, who didn't seem capable of seeing her, but at Nora, who was mouthing an apology when the Capitan put his hand behind her.

Again, he didn't touch her, but somehow the cool palm was a pressure and she moved wherever it seemed to say move, which was in the direction, remarkably, of the party. She looked once over her shoulder at Yesenia, who was tugging out her earrings as she trundled down the hill in the direction of the bus stop, not even visible for all the lush trees and flowering bushes in the yard. She stopped walking only once, to throw something twinkling over a fence.

The pimpled soldier stood outside the guard shack once again, struck a rigid stance and saluted.

Nora was confused. She tried saluting back.

"As you were," the Capitan shouted without turning.

Nora, striving hard to keep up with his wide stride, hid the gesture she'd mistakenly made by pointing out a hummingbird nosing a lily. "Pretty."

Higher up the hill, the city of Las Playas unfolded itself all the way to the ocean, the many palms like pins in a map. The most shifting piece of that map, the coastline, where a white veil tugged aside to reveal the shore, was also in a way the most dependable, had been there before the riots and the gang wars, the recession, the revolution, and the military reaction. So easy not to think of any of that anymore, strolling as Nora was by her Capitan's side. At the porch, bright fruit and bubbling drinks waited on tables in the shade. All the people moved fluidly among each other, laughing—at what jokes she was so eager to know she gripped his forearm tightly and he patted her hand twice. Nora felt the two of them would soon have jokes of their own at which to laugh, but tension worked through her ribcage to her stomach. She had a hard time finding interest in the people she met—a blur of faces and heady perfumes, the men and the women—and the whole evening seemed nothing but varying degrees of light changing the hues of the Capitan's thin mustache, making pleasant flourishes whenever he spoke. The gap between our society and this one felt more tangible to her than it ever had before. It felt physiological, a shrinking rib cage, crushing her out of existence in the interest of saving her from shame.

"I'll take you home," he said, at the end of the night, and gripped her elbow. She was shaky. He asked, "What is it?"

She looked across the yard at an old couple carrying their tuxedoed Pomeranian around the grounds.

He smiled and nodded. "Money doesn't buy anyone charm."

Something in his hazel eyes expanded her, staved off collapse. He took her hand and led her to the small, square rose garden on the west side of the house. "Money doesn't buy them looks, either. If it did, I'd have guessed you royalty."

The truth of her minimal status was so near the surface now that she could only submerge it by conscious force, a lie she was unwilling to tell. "You lay it on thick," she said. "But you should know—"

"I'll take you home."

She said again, "You lay it on real thick."

He straightened his jacket, a fitted thing that matched his slacks. "No. No. Not like that." He set his face to stone. Said coyly, "I'm only doing my duty. You're a citizen here, after all, and I'm responsible for you."

"There are thousands of citizens, Captain."

He smiled. Shook his head as if he'd entirely forgotten that fact. "Not like you. Where do you live?"

She stiffened. The crushing feeling returned to her stomach.

He seemed to notice the bad things at work inside her, and strolled over to a table littered with the remnants of the buffet. "I'll tell you something I do," he said. "But you can't tell anyone." He plucked a few chocolates, a grape, a cookie, from the table, wrapped them all in a napkin. He nodded at more of the leaving guests, their procession of laughter. "I'm not starving, but I'm not like them. And besides, they're going to throw it all out anyway." He slid the small white package into his inside coat pocket. "A chocolate?" he asked, offering her several choices in his flat palm.

"A Sellers woman never turns down sweets." She smiled, but when she raised her hand to pick out a chocolate they both realized he'd closed his fingers at the mention of her family name.

He promptly offered the chocolate again, and forced a smile.

"What's the matter?" She asked, pursing her lips and letting her pinched fingers hover above the chocolates in his hand.

But he was himself again. Hazel eyes, focused on her and beyond her at once, dark now, a green sea through which it was impossible to see what emotions cruised or darted. "Take one," he said. Then, firmly, "Go on."

Fourteen

The whole neighborhood sent off our children as messengers. When Leticia opened her door that evening, the woven smells of stew heavy like a curtain over her doorway, more than ten dusty children—most of them barefoot, the boys shirtless and the girls in boys' tee-shirts—warbled the news. Rudy had been taken by the military.

Our children begged Leticia not to go. We'd instructed them not to let her. She tried once, but she couldn't wade through the tangle of limbs at the front door. When she'd tried to sneak out back through her bedroom window, the older boys were hanging in her avocado tree and gibbering like monkeys. They gnawed on the green fruit, speaking through mushy mouths about the dangers for women who go seek their men in the jails. Telling her sometimes they never return.

Now she sat on the soft bed, leaned against the corner post, lean and knobby as her husband.

When Nora came in and went to the windows to draw the curtains tighter, outside the many eyes shut tight or flew off like moths. Children's voices flitted round the house, nested in the eaves. If Nora didn't tell her mother the whole story soon, Leticia would hear it through us.

Nora went to her mother, stroked her hair. She told her she'd read in a book on grief that it was best not to withhold information that may or may not be pertinent to the situation. She explained, still stroking her mother's hair—dark black and long and swept into a braid between her shoulder-blades—that knowing everything at once may seem harder at first, but in the end it allows one to reach each stage of grief with a firm footing. And, after all, what did they know right now but a few shady facts that may at any moment be illuminated by one bright truth.

"Mija." Leticia gripped Nora's hand. "My beautiful girl. Please, please-please, shut your mouth. You remind me too much of your father."

Nora pulled her hand away, massaging her mother's grip out of it. "Someone came after dad the day of his speech. A plomero."

"Plomero?" Leticia didn't go outside enough, or read papers or watch TV, to know all that went on. She found it easier to stay inside her home, and clean already clean things, and dream of her family in another country.

"One of those hired guns." Nora lowered the hand she'd foolishly raised in the shape of a pistol, and held her hands behind her back.

"Why didn't you tell me?" Leticia resented how much Nora and Rudy had in common: their reading, their place in that world outside.

"He thought it might have been Tre."

"My Tre?" Leticia asked.

Nora nodded.

Leticia slapped Nora once and pulled her hand instantly back to her lap.

Nora bit her lip. "I think we can figure this out."

Leticia gathered the thin blanket about her shoulders. She stood and went to the windows. The room was simple and mainly empty but the blanket dragged paperback books along the floor, books that Rudy may have been reading months ago and forgotten beneath the edge of the bed. Leticia slid each curtain open, first one side, then the other. Outside, all the older boys had herded the other children away from the windows, and they looked eager to hear some news they could take back to their own houses.

Leticia strung her hair over the front of one shoulder and began undoing her braid. "Tell your parents I'm doing what they should do. What all of us should do." She had the braid entirely unraveled and was ironing the kinks out of her hair with flat pressed palms.

Nora came to stand behind her mother. She looked curious, more than worried.

Without turning, Leticia said, "You're too much like your father for me to hear you talk right now." She looked again out the window at the dirt-streaked, ashy-legged congregation. Their slack mouths meant that they were listening, but their enormous eyes pretended to study the green bulbs of the tree. "Even the fruit makes me want to cry."

Leticia left her hair alone and gathered the blanket up like a robe, slowly, and slid off to the bathroom. She closed the door behind her, locked it from the inside while Nora watched the door in silence.

"Mom? Come out."

"What's the point?" the mother called.

When Nora turned back to the window it was empty of children. Avocado peels and their big brown seeds littered the ground outside. Her father's books littered the floor within. She began to stack them in her crossed arms like firewood. Eventually, she left them towered against the bathroom door. She wanted some way of knowing if her mother came out.

Fifteen

In a tremendous warehouse somewhere near the docks, the military kept Rudy with a few other bookish types in something like a giant fish tank. Glass walled them in on all sides, and from within you could not hear what was said outside, and from outside you could observe everything clearly, everything that went on within.

Not that much went on at all. The prisoners were ill-equipped to do much of anything but talk, and that they were afraid to do because of what we'd all heard were the typical prisoners' fates. Rudy knew all there was to know about the reputation of the jails, had helped to get a collection of personal accounts published in London, inspired by his research of the Russian tamizdat literature published abroad only to be smuggled back into the motherland. The prisoners in the fish tank were anything but typical or desperate, himself included.

The fish tank was overfilled with furniture; not a single wall didn't have a couch or a chair or a desk pushed against it, and there were three prisoners to hold it all down: Rudy, a woman named Maggie, and a young man named José. Maggie had been a journalist in her life outside, but that was two years ago. She'd been jailed after ignoring warnings that her editorials would get her killed. The editorial pieces did not take the side of the guerillas, but did not condemn them either, and most incriminatingly they indicted corrupt government for the grip drug lords held on the masses. Even now she smiled and scribbled into a notepad and said she was fortunate they hadn't killed her. She had grown so grateful, in fact, that she was nurturing romance with one of the officers who visited nightly, with the sound of his starched uniform like leaves shifting, and she left breezily for hours at a time. Her new scribbles were one part political commentary and two parts love sonnet, stanza blocks built down the pages that formed weeks worth of blocks of their own on the table.

José, who read the newspapers they were given no matter how outdated, had been a guerilla, and he wore his patchy beard proudly, kept his chin elevated at all times to show it off. He'd pointed fingers when his mother was jailed. They'd let him take her place.

Rudy chose to see the irony of his captivity as amusing, and looked around the fish tank smiling that mournful smile that said he was thinking. Lately, his inspiration for essays had come from the oddest of places. Using the Russian tamizdat for the idea to publish abroad: that had been an easy source to cite, an easy leap of logic. But now he was reading a bird book, and it had gotten him to thinking of Coleridge's albatross. He'd begun to suspect himself of yielding to the too obvious pressure to rest his thesis on the Mariner's violent assault, the crossbow shot that killed the bird and cursed the ship. That wouldn't do at all. He refused to let himself feel too much like a victim, but more to the point he wouldn't make the mistake of thinking there were such things as martyrs. A bolt through his heart would never deprive any ships' sails of their winds. Migration as natural and free, yes, rather than the doomed action of a desperate people. He wanted to find his way to a metaphor for flight.

The only space in the tank not blocked by furniture was the door, also glass, which occasionally let a colonel or captain through to join the three brains in some discussion of politics. The three, Maggie, José, and Rudy, vocally agreed with the military men—most of them fat old men with fat mustaches—no matter how simplistic their arguments or convoluted their logic, and the military men never seemed to mind, no matter how obvious the placation. They were all like that but one. The young Capitan with the hazel eyes.

The first day he entered the fish tank he brought their requested books, good tobacco, and rolling papers. He set them all on the edge of the desk, aligned the corners of the books with each other in a stack, then the bottom book with the corner of the desk itself. He told them as he fingered the scrollwork in the desk's wood that it had belonged to a labor union organizer whose communist leanings became increasingly obvious and they'd had to jail him. He complimented the man's taste enthusiastically. José sat up. He'd been reclining on the couch but now he sat hovering above it like a dirty toilet. Smirking, he asked, "The couch was his too?"

Maggie and Rudy sat at the desk, and they both studied the complex pattern of notes Rudy had prescribed to her sonnets. José went back to reading a newspaper with only some sections removed by the military, and that done courteously so as not to ruin the others. He peeked an eye through an empty square at the Capitan and offered a compatriotic wink to Rudy, who tried not to smile.

"Need anything else?" the Capitan asked.

They all shook their heads.

"Please, let us know if you do."

"How long will we be here?" Rudy asked.

"I can't say."

Rudy tapped the books stacked on the table. "Will this be enough books?"

The Capitan clutched his hands together behind his back. "I'm afraid not, for a reader like you." He took a step forward.

"You've been watching me. How long?"

"Don't feel too bad." The Capitan put a warm heavy palm on Rudy's shoulder. "These days, we watch everybody. I'll see if I can get some more books. Okay?"

Rudy blinked behind his glasses. He removed them to scrub them with his shirt, and to avoid the Capitan's eyes.

Other times the Capitan came late at night. The only lights on were those kept on the distant wide walls of the warehouse, and seen through the glass like quivering torches. Rudy always sensed the Capitan before he entered. Often, the Capitan stood outside the glass door, just a dark shape of a man, with one arm crossed and the elbow of the other resting on it, holding up his head. Like he needed that arm to support the weight of the thoughts going on inside.

Rudy didn't like to stir when the Capitan appeared. He enjoyed pretending to be asleep on the couch. José's snores and Maggie's occasional moans from dreaming about her boyfriend, the colonel, were the only sounds. Rudy enjoyed it because he knew the Capitan thought he was asleep and, while studying—scrutinizing—gave one a feeling of power, scrutinizing the scrutinizer was more complex. The Capitan was different when he wasn't putting on his show. Sometimes the Capitan shook his head. Sometimes his shoulders shuddered. Sometimes he just stared endlessly into the glass room, his eyes wide with wonder, Rudy wondering at what.

Once, the Capitan came in the early morning followed by a stiff assistant, a young soldier with a throat red from a close shave, and a tape player in his hands. The prisoners had already been led handcuffed through the morning toilet ritual, and all three sat at the desk. Rudy tongued the aseptic toothpaste lingering on his gums, and traded his coffee cup hand to hand to rub his raw wrists.

"A few questions," the Capitan said. Rudy had noticed that the Capitan was fond of beginning discussion this way. Not by asking, but by speaking as if the discussion were bound to begin. Rudy admired that about the young man. After all, Rudy's manner of speech was a slow, deliberate one, and anytime he was asked to speak for an occasion he labored over blank sheets of paper into the nights before. The Capitan seemed to move on instinct, except for when he was watching them late at night. This morning, the Capitan's eyes were dark and the eyelids heavy. The skin of his face lacked its luster and edge.

"You say it," he told the young soldier.

"But, Sir?"

"Say it," the Capitan said flatly, pressing a button on the tape recorder in the young soldier's arms.

The young soldier said, "Why are you here?"

Rudy, Maggie, José, all looked at each other and back at the Capitan's shiny black shoes. The Capitan ordered the young soldier: "Tell them."

"You are here because this country is diseased. There is concern that you are contributors to the disease."

The Capitan stared at them and for a moment he and Rudy exchanged arches of their eyebrows that spoke of those nighttime vigils. Rudy thought maybe the Capitan recognized something familiar in the moment. The Capitan shook his head, sighed. Looked more tired by the minute.

The young soldier went on. "When a man has gangrene in the leg, we must eliminate the leg to save the man. Understand? It is like you are in quarantine."

The Capitan watched the tape player the young soldier held stiffly before his stomach. As the tape wound round, its motor made a ticking like a clock. The Capitan moved his mouth to speak, but said nothing, and blinked several times. The young soldier was saying, "If we find that you are diseased, we will do our best to cure you."

"Your best?" José smiled. "That's heartwarming."

By now the Capitan's eyes had that lost look of someone in need not just of sleep, but also of rest, of escape. He pressed a button on the player and the young soldier swayed—out of nervousness or the weight of the Capitan's hand, you couldn't tell. The tape rewound a moment and the Capitan pressed another button that produced again that white empty space that meant what was said was being recorded. The young soldier repeated dutifully, "We will do our best to cure you. We will operate on the diseased pieces." When he'd finished, the young soldier beamed, proud to have remembered it all.

The Capitan said, "Now. The three of you say that you understand."

They said they did.

"Louder. Say your name and that you understand."

They did. The Capitan left the young soldier struggling to turn off the tape player, which he couldn't seem to figure out under the weight of the captives' presence.

"You." The young soldier pointed at Rudy. "You know these things?"

"If it weren't for those things, my biggest fan would have no record of my lectures. So, yes, I know them very well."

"Get up here and turn it off."

José held again the cut-up newspaper, his leg draped over the chair's arm. When he raised the paper his lips and beard filled the space where the editorial ought to have been.

In response to the young soldier's order, Rudy lowered his glasses onto the sharp bridge of his nose, returned to reading sonnets: a gesture that everyone in the room felt as magnified, contorted like the reflected words in his bifocals, and into something quite significant.

The young soldier struggled more with the player, finally ejected the tape and tucked it into his pocket. He gripped the player in both hands.

José was now grinning proudly at Rudy through the space of the editorial when the soldier stepped off to one side, looked on the verge of striking Rudy but, stopped by some order like an unseen hand on his shoulder, instead swung the player through the paper into José's mouth.

José sprawled backwards with the chair to writhe in the pages plastered to his face.

The soldier looked at the player in his hands, which was now cracked along one side. On the table, beside Rudy's books, a plastic shard spun like a beetle on its back.

"Damaging government property." The young soldier locked a heel back, about faced, and went, saying, "I'll have to report this."

José stripped the paper from his face, cursed, and spat blood.

Maggie took her notepad up and began scribbling. "You know what they meant, don't you?" she said, not even looking up. "About the diseased piece?"

She kept tapping out meter on her temple.

"Yes. That's what they mean." Rudy took up a book. "But the Capitan, he's different."

José tugged at a front tooth, lisping, "Your disease is hope, man. That's the worst one."

Rudy smiled, his eyes looking through an imaginary doorway, looking in on his sleeping daughter. "I'm my daughter's father."

Sixteen

We saw the Capitan around their house every evening, at first just tiptoeing outside the window. Occasionally, his forearms leaned onto the sill to talk to the girl. Nora wouldn't leave the house as long as her mother was still locked inside. And besides that she was waiting for whenever her brother finally returned home; it had already been a few weeks. But the Capitan assured her that her father was safe and healthy and would be released soon.

He dressed impeccably, his shirts starched to the verge of cracking. He refused himself to stand or lean in any posture not already deemed worthy by some statue he'd seen in a square or museum. Beneath his shirts and pants was a weavework of garters and snaps and straps that kept all creases creased and all drapes draped and all tucks tucked however his posturing for Nora taxed them. Because of Nora's view from the window she could not see his careful picking at the elastic straps in his clothes.

The neighborhood boys who walked the walls half naked began posturing too. From her bedroom window Nora could watch this retinue of mimes perched on the wall over the Capitan's shoulder. When he turned to see them they made a game of jumping off the wall to the alley behind. Their feet slapped loudly on the asphalt.

The Capitan, puzzled at her smile, stroked her cheek with the backs of his fingers. "Your father's fine. He wants you to know that he's reading Márquez. Can I come in now, my little bird?"

He'd recently begun to call her by these sorts of names and she liked it. He rarely used the same one two days in a row.

Her cheek flushed under his hand. "Why do you call me that?"

"You're a beautiful thing and you're trapped in that cage. Now, can I come in after you?"

She looked around her bedroom. It looked clean in the pink brilliance through the window, but it smelled dusty and yellow like old pages. Her books were stacked in towers around the room, towers she could look down on like a lost city much quieter than any she knew. She stood on her bed to reach the window with the ease the Capitan bore naturally by height and thick-soled shoes. He could pass through the window with ease too, she thought.

No. She couldn't have a man in the house. Her father wouldn't approve and her mother was perhaps going insane and it was…well, it was all pretty embarrassing. "And you're sure he's okay?"

He nodded.

"Have they done anything to him?"

"I can't say that." He thumbed her hair past her cheek, her ear.

"Have they?"

"They've been easy on him, compared to the others. But he'll be out soon."

"How soon?"

"I don't know. Can't I come in?"

"Soon."

"When?"

"When will he be out?"

When the Capitan said, "I'll come back when I know more," Nora sighed and sucked in the cool air blowing her curtains against her blushing cheek.

Seventeen

Tre sliced the razor halfway through the shell shaped cartilage before he passed out, the razor left lodged in the young man's ear.

The young man stopped screaming long enough to watch Tre with a look of morbid indignance as he crumpled to the ground, fainted. Their victim even managed to kick Tre once before the others dragged away the chair to which he was tied. The others began slapping Tre in the face to wake him. "Pussy," they called Tre. "Just a little blood," one said. "Don't you earn your stripes from your girl once a month?" asked another.

Tre elbowed himself partway up and shook his head clear. "First off, she's prettier than this dude, and we ain't talking about ears. Second? There's gotta be a better way to get money."

The young men surrounding Tre were shaking their heads and jabbing each other.

"Yeah," Junior, the biggest, said. "Let's just send the parents a card and ask for it. We'll spray a little perfume. I bet you got some."

"Fuck you. I say we go back to hits."

"You're just dizzy. It's no money in hits." Junior blew into a plastic lined envelope in one hand, shaking a pen in the other. "Anyway, you said you were done with hits." He leaned over to the young man in the chair, "What's your parents' address?"

The young man tied to the chair was crying. He kept saying ow and he sounded like a little boy. "Please don't," he shouted. "Please."

Standing, Tre wiped his hands on the legs of his pants. "That's cause we're hitting the wrong people. Let's start hitting the right ones."

The "right ones," to Tre's mind, were the men who had sent him after his father. They were politicos, they were corrupt military officials, they were warring guerilla factions wanting to blame the politicos or the corrupt military officials for hits. And they all had dirty money Tre could think to put to better use. Uses that the Negra approved of, so that now she'd see him whenever he wanted to see her, which was often.

That's when Tre began to make a name for himself. It was only a few weeks after he'd left home. The people in his girlfriend's neighborhood liked him for his motorbike and for the money he sometimes gave them or the toys he gave their kids. When his girlfriend, the Negra, would sit in bed counting his cash into a jar, he swooped in and yanked the jar from between her legs and put his face there instead. He kissed the stitching of her jeans and tugged the cold zipper with his front teeth.

She laughed. She was always laughing once he moved in with her. They made a game of hot potato with the jar but in the end he took the cash out and went to spend it on good food.

Sometimes they had three courses. They often invited all the neighboring families to the Negra's hut and people had to bring their own dishes or else eat out of bowls made from aluminum foil. Some of the neighbors brought guitars and buckets to play like drums. They got drunk on liquor that the Negra made from the subsidized sugarcane that overtook the yards years ago when the recession hit and no one could afford to keep grass.

In bed, at the end of the night, she stared solemnly into the empty glass jar. He looked at her through the other side, her almond eyes like wide leaves or a captured moth clapping wings when she blinked.

She was older than he, and she got tired sooner. He was a little drunk and feeling playful and he cupped the curve where her ass met her thigh, his cock murmuring awake at her knee. Sometimes, like now, she slept frowning. "Stop now." Her lips parted on a breath instead of words, and he knew by the wetness on his thumb-knuckle she meant stop the work, not the touching.

"Look it. I could die any day. What good will the money do me then?"

"You could do other work." She didn't bother opening eyes, though their lids fluttered.

"What other work?"

"We could sell my liquor around the other barrios."

"And get put in jail? No thanks. Rather the reaper."

He pinched her butt and she didn't bat his hand away, just said he had poetry in his blood, and turned her back to him. He stroked her belly a few times and pulled her to him but when he started kissing her neck she was already breathing like sleep. He sighed, reached underneath the bed, and produced a sketchpad and pencil. Then he started in on a fresh page.

Eighteen

When the women of the neighborhood heard about Leticia's protest, they went to see for themselves. They waited down the street until Nora went to classes—a small mob of middle-aged and elderly women with hotplates and pastries, candles and flowers in hand. To seem less conspicuous they chatted about whatever first crossed their minds, but Nora remarked once that all the women were getting a little senile because she heard one woman tell another that the weather was fine, and the response had come: that's because the boyfriend turned out to be a fairy and never slept in the marriage bed.

As soon as Nora passed in the car, the women scuttled around back of the house. The gate was kept locked, and the women gave each other boosts over the fence. The ones that were too old or too weak to manage passed their treats over the fence and sulked off down the alley. We often heard Sally complain that her dress was ripped or that she'd had to scrub it twice to get the shoeprints out of it. She was the only one large enough to support their weight with ease. Getting herself over the wall required just as much effort on the part of the others, who had to sit on top of the wall and tug while she treaded her way up the concrete barefoot. Her feet were like a cat's, dead leather at the bottoms, and she left her chanclas down in the alley whenever they all went to see Leticia.

"Leticia," they singsonged at the bathroom window tucked into the patio, where ferns and air plants hung from hooks and made a shady maze of green.

Sally was the only one tall enough to peer inside the window and she did, put a finger to her mouth and said, "She's asleep."

"What do we do?" one of the women asked.

"We wait," Sally said.

"Why not wake her up?" another asked, her head pushed forward by the whisper.

"Her husband is in jail after her own son tried to kill him. Her daughter is seeing that Captain behind her back. Now she's living in a bathroom in a house in our neighborhood in this country. I think she needs her rest."

All of the other women nodded their heads at that. They sat down in a circle because they were tired of their hair catching in the hanging plants, and they waited.

Nineteen

"Professor Sellers?" The Capitan stood before the open glass door, waiting. "Will you come with me now?"

Rudy pinched the creases of his slacks, which had held up well considering he'd sweated into them for the last few weeks. When he stood he gripped his lapels, tugged the collar of his coat down once, and nodded.

"Professor Sellers?"

Rudy stood at the desk, stroking his chin. "I can't choose."

The Capitan said, "Rudy?"

Rudy turned. It was the first enlistment of either one by the other, and both men were relieved when Rudy returned to the books. The Capitan wouldn't rush him now. "I've read Márquez, but he's so good I don't want to use him up. My daughter loves him, but I've always meant to read Faulkner, too."

"This one," the Capitan said, touching with two fingers the finch on the cover.

"That's an old one. I've read it through."

"It won't be like last time. It'll be nice to have a few pretty pictures."

"What is it today, then?"

"A few questions."

"Why don't you ask them here?" Rudy smiled around the room, but his peers didn't meet his eyes. José, as usual, hiding behind a newspaper. Maggie, as usual, hiding behind the poetry in her mind. As usual, all the different kinds of hiding.

The Capitan said, "It's not me asking."

"Oh." Rudy stuttered a finger down the bindings of the stacked books. José folded up the paper and set it in his lap. Maggie had been scribbling, and stopped.

"I see," Rudy said. "No. Not the one you suggested. The Márquez then, but after I get back. Nora loves Márquez."

A smile creased the Capitan's eyes.

From outside the fish tank, the sound of the shutting door drummed.

The Capitan walked off, and Rudy took a moment before following. Women sat at desks arranged in neat long rows, typing, desk lamps haloing their hair. In one corner of the warehouse a few officers stood pinching their fingers on the ribbons of their cigarette smoke. They were laughing at a joke Rudy missed.

He must have passed the cells where they kept the other prisoners. Must have passed rooms full of knees against concrete for days on end, heads lolled inside of grain sacks, and Rudy must have felt fortunate. Maybe grateful, like Maggie was to her new lover the colonel who'd raped her, but only the first time. Rudy must have heard the sounds of torture that wandered through that cement maze. He must have wondered, even hoped because they treated him well by comparison; he must have had faith in his keepers that they would see reason and let him loose.

We've all heard the stories, and he must have known them too. What with all his reading, his writings, his research. Iron bands on beds, chairs, and two hundred and twenty volts, enough for a man's eyes to light up even the darkest room. Vices, god-knows-what crushed inside them. Impossibly clean and coldly gleaming instruments. Things for cutting, and different things for puncturing. Sand-bags for beating.

At some point, though, Rudy chose to believe that the Capitan was not responsible for this, that Rudy must have been handed over to Intelligence. He must have been put in the quiet chamber alone. They probably tied him to something, but they might have left him free. Either way they asked him questions the way they asked all prisoners questions. In one of his papers, Rudy had written about a pregnant woman who'd had her fetus shocked with a spoon attached by a short wire to a car battery. So Rudy knew about the things they did. We imagined it might have been harder on him for that reason: because he knew. Better it all were a mystery. But Rudy sat in that cell and waited for specifics, maybe trying not to imagine some cold chunk of steel gleaming through the doorway, coming closer to his skin as he curled up, shrunk away, tried to blink from sight. He listed all his options again and again, because he was like that. He listed drowning, and cutting, and stabbing, and beating, and swelling, and electric shock, and he picked one. He must have. There must have been one he would take over any other. Hoping for the shock. Or for the beating. Hoping for the cuts over anything else.

The Capitan held the glass door open, waiting. With his tight lips he did not look pleased and, while he didn't direct his anger at any of the prisoners, his eyes were wild with it.

Rudy tried to maintain his trademark posture, but his stiff back only increased the shambling nature of his steps. He paused, caught his breath. A gurgling sound in the nose and throat. He wouldn't raise his head, wouldn't look at anyone. When Rudy had finally entered the fish tank the Capitan said that now that they could be sure he'd told the truth it was only a matter of time. He said it wouldn't be much longer, and said this more times than he had to. He seemed to feel that condolence, like everything else in life, was a matter of momentum, and before he could stop himself he told Rudy that he would send Nora his love.

"Oh." Rudy looked up. Rudy couldn't care too much now, about the Capitan and Nora. "I see." His nose had been crushed to one side, pillowed and purple. "Not a word about this, then."

The Capitan blushed at his slip up, rushed out.

The door closed and the Capitan dissolved beyond the glass. Rudy wanted to keep the notes in his head in order, but each painful blink shuffled the words and pictures at random. The gruff voices. The worn tools. The dank smells. The only coherent thesis he had formed concerned the mutual conceit that occurred between humans in situations of distress. The feeling that the captor and captive were in trouble together. He thought of falcon and falconer, but then realized: in that figuration he was only a pigeon.

Maggie kept scribbling, but José went to the desk and slid the Márquez out of the stack. He led Rudy by an elbow to the couch. Maggie moved over, but wouldn't look at Rudy. She never got the business because she was fucking that colonel. One day they would discover that she was pregnant and the colonel would have the baby shocked. Maggie would eventually die on that couch in the fish tank, from the business she got, right where she was now, scribbling.

"You okay?" José put the book in Rudy's hands.

Rudy stroked the cover with his palm and it made a soothing sound that was loud in the glass walled room. He was weighing two sides of an argument, listening with each ear to a different voice.

Maggie set her pen on the pad.

Rudy looked at it, considered something that grabbed José and Maggie's attention. They both leaned toward Rudy a bit, expectant. Then Rudy looked away from the pen. "My wife tells me I read too much. We think it's ruining my eyes."

Twenty

Still the vicious sons of bitches were behind him. Tre fought to keep the motorbike straight in the road but the sack of cash on his back kept swinging him side to side. The bank guards hadn't been a problem, but the politico he'd caught in the middle of a transaction, and from whom he'd stolen a sack of diamonds that was stabbing the inside of his thigh through the inside of his pocket even now, had hired the private team of mercenaries lounging against the hoods of cars in the parking lot outside, casually passing a cigarette in a circle.

Now they were passing bullets Tre's way, and between the bullets and the bag and the rare lack of traffic to weave through, Tre was sweating and swearing, spit on his visor, heat fogging his vision as well as his thoughts. A bullet struck a stop sign just above his head. Anyway, this time, there was no time for thoughts.

He ducked the bike down an alley and twisted hard on the throttle. He burned through a puddle, tore that watery sun in half. His back, long soaked with sweat and alley water, ached and spasmed. And still they cornered their jeep down the alley behind him, jeering and laughing and launching more bullets.

He could turn left or right, down similar, wide, multi-lane streets, where his pursuers would have all the space in the world to catch up with him. There was no doubling back, because to show his side to them for even the instant it would take to flip a bitch would be like asking for a bullet in the gut or the fuel tank.

Straight ahead was the square, and it was too packed with people to see to its other side, and it was too packed with pigeons to see the peoples' feet. Where children ran to the broken fountain, birds rolled away in waves but never left the ground too long. The square belonged to them more than to the people of Clearwater.

It would take something bigger to scare them off.

He revved the bike through its gears, up-shifting the instant the needle bounced behind the glass. Still the bullets. Still the jeep's motor behind him roared.

The square was not silent, not even quiet, until the first stray bullet chipped a chunk off the fountain, felled the toe from the lost politico's stone loafer.

One bird pecked at the rock-chips on the ground. The fat grey one beside it turned up a round black eye. An old man, on a bench beside the fountain, lowered his newspaper, looked around, and raised it again. Then the first woman of many cried out, and ran off with her child.

Tre didn't slow at all. He took the shift from asphalt to cobbles with barely a small burp in his belly, and thumbed the horn in staccato chirps. Men women and children scattered. With no direction to go but up, the birds took flight together, hundreds of them, a curtain Tre was sure he'd never pass through.

Shit hit his visor in bursts of black and white. Wings fluttered against his arms, closing in, overwhelming him. But soon a feathered corridor opened. A brief glimpse at daylight opening its own wings beyond.

Until he caught a fat-bellied bird with the side-view, and lost the sun and the side-view skittering on the ground out of sight, almost losing his balance as well. Then, just when he'd thought he'd been swallowed, the corridor burst and the sky flared wide, the square empty of all but the old man still watching him tentatively above a newspaper.

Tre nodded his head when he passed, and the old man went back to the news.

Tre swung out of the square with the rear tire leading. Stuttered a foot on the asphalt to balance. He cut right down an alley, and this got him far enough that he could hazard a glance back. Needed to. Because there was no open end to this alley. Just a tall brick wall.

Shit painted his visor, fingers slipping as he tried to lift it, but he finally gave up and ripped the helmet away.

His eyes flicked to any movement at all: laundry on the line above, crippled dog in a doorway, water running from a spigot into a glass jar at the corner of the alley.

There.

In the glass jar: a growing cloud of color.

It hadn't worked, he thought. They'd seen him. And now they'd find him, back to a wall, no better than a man facing the firing squad. And for what? A few diamonds, maybe just chunks of glass, for all he knew.

The globe of color in the jar exploded when the jeep rushed past the small framed space of Tre's alley. A few of the men kept their pistols aimed ahead. Most, though, were picking feathers from their hair and mouths.

Tre waited, chuckling, and long after he heard their engine fade out, his laughter was loud in the small alley, and even he didn't know where it came from. Still, he couldn't stop smiling. There wasn't any reason to stop. No. There was always something to smile about, these days.

Tre opened throttle out of the alley, passed the now empty square, and out into the surrounding barrio. Here he found the dirt path through the sugarcane, the path he'd built, and the most direct one to his girl's house.

Well maybe he hadn't built it himself, but it was there because of him. He'd paid the teenagers two bucks each to clear the path and it had taken them a whole day. Their shoulders had been red with sun when they returned nodding their heads up and down and saying We did it, we did it, nearly dragging Tre out of the yard to see. The Negra had been boiling cane in the kitchen. Now the road and its rattling cane walls made him think of her and how her fingers always smelled like sugar and between her legs like sea. He came to a stop where the dirt was soft beneath the tires and where the air was cool and smelled good.

The boys jockeyed to be the first to bring the tarp out to him. They outright fought when he said one of them could walk the motorbike to the shed and cover it and lock the door. He pushed them apart and pointed at the thin one, Ricardo, and pointed at the shed. The tall chubby one was named Dale. Dale got to cover the bike and lock the door shut.

When Tre entered the kitchen the Negra said from the stove, "Your father was looking for you."

He set the sack of cash and the helmet on the table. "Here? What'd he look like?"

"Big."

"Do I look like I come from big men?"

In response, she slumped her shoulders closer to the heat of the stove, as if she were looking for some comfort in its warmth. "I told you."

"Don't worry." He took the diamonds out of his pocket and snuck up behind her, covered her eyes with one hand. "I got you something."

He dropped the diamonds in the boiling sugar and pushed her aside. Told her to keep her eyes closed. She didn't. She never listened to him. She smiled and watched him fish through the soupy mixture with a strainer.

"Close your eyes," he said. She laughed and closed them. "Don't swallow," he said, blowing on a diamond in his hand. "Abrela."

She opened her mouth, stuck out her tongue, and once he'd set the diamond there she pulled it in. Her lips pursed and her cheeks caved and she shut her eyes tight and moaned.

"What do you think?" he asked.

She spat the diamond into her palm and her eyes popped wide. Big, round, white. "Delicioso, pero..."

He took her face in his hands. "And if I put it on a ring?"

She put the diamond back in his hand. "It still wouldn't be mine. Not the way you're mine. Not the way I'm yours."

He closed his hand around it. "I see."

Twenty-One

We couldn't blame Nora for seeing the Capitan. She was in a very sensitive state. She was taking as good care of her mother as her mother would allow, but that wasn't much. Nora set food by the door, but the door never opened. Eventually the flies buzzed so much that Nora heard them from her own bedroom and would come in and clear the plates and open all the windows. The mosquitoes glided in through the windows at night, so she stopped bringing the food and her mother didn't seem to notice. Dust tufted the door's bottom.

"Aren't you hungry?" Nora called through the door.

Her mother's voice echoed, "I'm eating my heart."

The bathroom made her sound hollow, and Nora almost believed her. Actress, she thought. Drama queen.

Nora didn't know about the women and their pastries visited down through the window each day. Leticia ate better in that bathroom than she ever had before because her own cooking had become so bland after years of living with Rudy and his sensitive digestion, his unremarkable income. She'd gained at least two pounds the first week. And two the next. She was fortunate to have been wearing a dress when she locked herself inside, which she scrubbed in the sink and hung over the towel rack by noon, so it would be dry when the cool evenings came to chill the small box of tile and porcelain.

Nora sat outside the door on a pillow, reading aloud her favorite passages from Maugham, Faulkner, Márquez and Rulfo.

"Will you stop that?" her mother said.

Nora often bit her nails and puzzled over the strange change in her mother's voice—it sometimes sounded as if her mouth were full to bursting, though that was impossible.

"They're beautiful passages."

"Can't you tell me something about real people? Don't you have any friends?"

"I met someone."

"For a girl who reads so much you tell an awful story."

"I met a man."

"No," Leticia exclaimed. "Who is he?"

"He's a Captain. In the Navy."

The door shot open into Nora's rear, shooting her up onto her feet with a shriek, and slammed shut again. "Read to me more, Mija," Leticia said. "I don't like your stories."

Nora read her the last piece of Faulkner's The Hamlet, where the men dig all night for the treasure, only to learn it's worth nothing in the end. Leticia giggled. She coughed and sucked in air, then laughed loudly, once. Soon her laughter was rolling around the bathroom tiles so that from the bedroom it sounded like the bathroom was full of women. Leticia shushed someone. Outside, where Nora could not see, Sally raised a fat fist that silenced all the women chatting beneath the hanging plants on the patio.

"Mama?" Nora called against the bathroom door.

"Yes?"

"Are you okay?"

"Mmhm. Keep reading, Mija. I like this Falcon guy."

"You tell me a story now." Nora lay out a few more pillows and curled up in front of the door. She used a book as a pillow because she liked its smell, a timid but fibrous smell she associated with her father—like a thin, but a strong, rope. Her mother would speak nothing of her father. And not much about herself, or even Nora. By Nora's analysis, the rest of the family seemed only tributaries that fed into the river of Tre. Leticia told Nora how when she carried Tre in her belly he punched and kicked her so hard she wanted him out. So she put a finger in her belly button and said I'm going to count to three and you're going to come out of me. And she counted. And when she got to three she knew it had worked, and her water broke. But then she sniffed the air and cursed, because Tre had only kicked the pee out of her. He stayed in almost a month too long.

Nora thought, right before sleep sapped her of her thoughts, that she heard her mother crying in the bathroom, crying for her baby boy, and for her husband, and even for Nora too, and she dreamed a larger river separating again, into many small streams that seeped into the earth's hollows. The strange thing was that many women's voices joined her mother's in a chorus. Nora woke up with a dry mouth, in the silence of the night in a nearly empty house, a song or a prayer or consolation in her ears.

Then it was good dreams. A dream about her family in a nice home, in a nice city, somewhere near the beach. Rudy, Leticia, Tre, Nora. They were all together and they were all happy, except for Nora, who was sad because her Captain was somewhere left behind, and she slunk behind the rest dragging her feet in the clean white sand.

So you see, it was in this sensitive state that she saw the Capitan again. Any of us, young, in the worst kind of love there is—the kind which family and society and class all agree cannot be—would have done the same thing. Maybe worse. She went out the window to him, telling herself that the daylight made it an okay thing to do. At least she didn't have him in the house.

She'd been reading to her mother, who was occasionally laughing and whispering in hushed tones at parts in the stories that warranted no laughter, and Nora was very concerned that her mother was going slowly crazy. She remembered the strange ladies gathered down the street each time she left the house, and how crazy they'd seemed. She resolved to go straight to the library and research any forms of mental illness or senility that might be contagious or related to menstruation, perhaps menopause, maybe even related to diseases from the birds in the square, though she knew this was ridiculous and just an attempt to rationalize her fears. Then she heard a knock on her own bedroom window, set the book down on the floor, and crept off.

The Capitan was standing back from the window, bronzed by the sun. With his hands in his pockets he formed a formidable V from shoulders to waist. "Can I come in?"

"Has my father been let out?"

"I'm trying."

"I had a bad dream about a beach," she said. "You weren't there."

"That's impossible, Palomita." He reached his hand out and told her to come outside into the sun. That so much time indoors caused melancholy. She told him the true causes of melancholy, in alphabetical order, no less, then went red in the face, and slid one leg through the window.

They left out of the back yard and returned through it too. They were not gone too long, but something was different between them. With the tension over having him finally released, softening her, the doubts she'd kept submerged began to surface. "What should we do? My family? You and I?"

"I promise you," he said, while they made a game of weaving onto opposite sides of the blue sheets swelling on the laundry line. "It's a slow process, but it's a sure one. We do good work."

"Why do you need my dad? He's done nothing wrong." She stopped on one side of a sheet, he on the other. It was easier for her to say what she said without facing him. "I think you're lying."

He pulled the sheet free of the line and the wooden pins snapped into the air like cicadas, fell dead in the grass. "I'm trying to get him out."

"You're lying about doing good work, then."

He grabbed her wrist and she groaned in pain, and in an instant he was apologizing to her, kissing the white inside of her wrist. The blue sheet pooled at their feet, and they danced in it awkwardly, getting closer. This could have been the water at the beach of her dreams, and her Capitan there too.

"Tell me," she said. "Tell me what happens where you keep them."

He let go her wrist, crouched to gather up the sheet and the clothespins. The soft dreamy quality of things relented, hardened. Again, the world was a kiln. "Tell me."

He hung the sheet up between them, and he was larger suddenly, his shadow burned onto the sheet by the sun. He seemed swollen to something beyond his capacity, and that might burst into shards before her eyes, and she realized that if he was it was the fault of her own hope. When her heart had gotten its hottest and she thought her eyes would char from all the frustration she had not admitted to herself, and surely could not say, something rustled beneath the avocado tree, hummed in the shade and wind-shuffled leaves, emerged.

The five women that had been in the patio lumbered into the sun, shading their eyes with spotted hands. Sally's large feet were bare. She held her chanclas as usual, and she raised them to fan her face.

Nora couldn't see the Capitan's face through the sheet, but she sensed him looking at her for some sort of explanation. She had none. Her tongue was dry and numb. Her thoughts finally abandoned her, hid from life's heat, deep in a well of feeling. She did not know how to reclaim them. She closed her eyes to think of something rational to say, but nothing would come. When she opened them the women were shaking their heads.

The sheet billowed. The Capitan's shadow was gone, him along with it.

Twenty-Two

The day was bright white with sun, and windy. Palm trees creaked against telephone wires—seagulls and kites hovered over the shore. A small, cream convertible, with the top down, streamed down the curves of the road. Rudy's nose was still crooked but healing, and hardly needed the band-aid across the bridge, over which he now acknowledged the Capitan's precise face. Rudy felt his own thinning hair twisted in the wind but the Capitan's hair was immoveable, like it came out of a mold.

"I thought you'd enjoy a nice drive." The Capitan spoke out of the right side of his mouth and kept his eyes on the road at all times, with his hands at ten and two on the wheel. Though the seatback was reclined in a cavalier fashion, he hardly let his back touch it. "I know it's stifling back there." He cringed at his own reminder of the prison.

"Will I be out soon?" Rudy asked, almost cringing as well at his request for permission. "Or maybe my family can visit?"

"If your family visited then the other people, they'd get up in arms about their families too. It's best if we're consistent. But this," the Capitan gestured out at the sea, "no one knows about it. This is just for you."

"Thank you."

"Don't think about it. It's a strange job, and things like this help me. They help me to... I'm not sure, really. Isn't that funny?" The

Capitan jerked the small car around a tight curve, and the car darted toward the shimmering waters and small white waves of Sunset Beach. It was funny, to Rudy, that the Capitan seemed unsure of something. Especially now, clicking the radio on, then off again, checking the glove box for cigarettes, then tsking himself and leaving them be. Did his new insecurity have something to do with his slip about having seen Nora?

"Isn't it funny how we do a job and don't really know all its ins and outs? I've been wondering about your job. What's it like being a professor?"

Surfers stood at the water's edge with surfboards balanced atop their heads. The houses on either side were small, bright, and square.

Rudy asked, "Do you live in this neighborhood?"

"Me? Military men don't make this kind of money. We do what we do out of passion or—the men that live here, god knows what they do." He smiled. "You didn't answer my question. About being a professor."

Rudy couldn't decide what to do with his hands, and when he finally let one hang off the door to feel the wind, the Capitan beamed and took his eyes off the road just long enough to look at Rudy and laugh. The Capitan laughed with his head back, top teeth white and gleaming. "That's right. Enjoy yourself. You're a smart man. We need men like you. Tell me about some of your co-workers."

"The dean of English is a close friend of mine. We get together in the summers to make chili. Tut won a contest for best chili in Playas just last year."

"Best chili. That's something. And books? Does he read the same sorts of books as you?"

A woman returning from the ocean distracted Rudy. She padded to a yellow bungalow, dusted sand off her tan legs with a striped towel. He missed the weight of Leticia's leg over his own when they slept.

"The books, Dr. Sellers."

"Well, yes. We have that in common. We're both men of letters."

"Men of letters."

"Yes."

"And politics," the Capitan offered.

"Well, not politics, per se."

"Per se?"

"I mean, not exactly. You know I've given speeches on human rights."

"You have?"

"Yes. You know that."

"And this chili cook, he has too?"

"I don't know. Maybe. What I mean to say is that we aren't political activists or extremists, we're just ordinary men."

"Not just ordinary men, Dr. Sellers. Men of letters."

Rudy shifted in his seat.

The Capitan said, "Those are your words."

Rudy had been letting one hand float up and down with the windstream but he pulled it back inside and set it with the other in his lap. He kneaded one hand into the other.

The Capitan flipped his visor up when they turned away from the sea, past restaurants with couples seated at outdoor tables taking glinting bottles of beer from metal buckets.

"Relax, Dr. Sellers. I'm only asking questions. Maybe I should have taken another approach. I know you're nervous, but the more you participate, the sooner you'll be out. I want that as much as anybody. But, this job. It goes unappreciated. We're only looking for potential threats. No one understands that. We want to know that you, your family, are safe. That everyone's families are."

The freedom of the road reminded Rudy he was not free, and he pinched the tension high at the top of his nose, "You believe that? All the way up, they only want us safe? They don't want our money, or our land? Or our daughters?"

The Capitan mis-shifted and the gear growled. He jerked the shifter down into first. Their ride seemed to start over.

Rudy studied the pretty houses as they passed. "We won't be safe as long as we live here."

"Your wife wants to leave too, now."

"She wanted to from the beginning. I should have listened—" Rudy only stopped from facing the Capitan completely when the seatbelt locked against his shoulder. "How could you know that?"

The Capitan didn't look away. Rudy knew the Capitan was waiting for Rudy to drift, to show that he'd realized Nora's relationship with this man had grown intimate enough to share family secrets. It was impossible to tell if the car had crossed the line in the road. Whether or not it had, Rudy felt something dangerous and certain ahead of them, an impact. It didn't take Rudy long to look away from the Capitan to the open road, and then out to the green ocean in defeat. As a father, not just a man, he'd lost a contest here.

"So long as your son goes too. She told Nora." The Capitan went on, opening his hand on the stick-shift like it were a weapon, a gesture of peace. "Me, my friends, my coworkers, we're good people like you and yours. Give you my word. We aren't barbarians. We aren't the police or the guerillas. The people you see get hurt, it's because they give us no other choice. Nothing is going to happen to you or your family once all the evidence checks out. I can do that."

Rudy looked out at the horizon, where the pelicans dove in, white water, and rose again, silver light. American Whites. Pelecanus Erythrorhynchos. The fifteen-inch beak was vivid orange this time of year. Could carry so much. Rudy turned to the Capitan. "And what else can you do?"

The Capitan's near eyebrow arched, and he smiled. "I see."

Rudy sighed, nodding. He was testing the wind stream again with an open palm, wind feeling like tattered cloth between his fingers.

"Your friend. The chili cook," the Capitan said. "You'll have to tell me his name. And you'll have to give me some time to figure a way out for your family."

Rudy's face was grim, but, finally, the knot at his brow went slack with relief. "I've already got one. All of us, gone away, just like that."

Rudy flattened his palm into a wing and let it ride the cool wind out the window in crests and troughs. For a moment, he could imagine that wind carried the past away, was bringing something good and simple along with it. For all the rush in his ears, he hardly heard the Capitan say, "All except Nora, of course."

Twenty-Three

Once, at the llantería on the corner decorated with rusty hubcaps and dusty pillars of tires, Tre asked the old man called Viejo, with the flatbed truck, for a ride to the bank.

The old man in his cowboy hat looked around the empty yard, fists of grass punching through the pavement. A quiet corrido about an old love played for a man inside a lone car passing. A mangy dog stopped in the street to scratch its ear with a hind leg, showing them his prunish legacy. Viejo asked, "What if it gets busy?"

Tre handed over two dollars and Viejo showed brown teeth, removed his sweat-stained cowboy hat and smacked Tre on the shoulder with it. "I'll get the truck."

The bed was full of tires that made the truck creak like an old door and the street passed beneath the open holes in the floorboards.

"Where you going?" Tre asked.

"The bank."

"Not that one. Turn here and go to the one on Artesia."

"Okay. But why not the other one?" Viejo's yellowed eyes came from too much drink, but Tre couldn't think of any illness that made eye contact difficult. "You always go to the other one, no?" Viejo smiled again.

"Are you asking me, Viejo, or is the man with his hand up your ass asking now?"

"Qué?" Viejo said. "What you talking?"

At the bank, Tre walked up to the Sinestra teller and changed the cash. She didn't ask him if he wanted a receipt, didn't ask for I.D.—one of the few newer laws that worked in Tre's favor. It took the teller ten minutes to count it all out. When she was done she pushed neat stacks to him one at a time through the slot, which he dropped into the same dirty sack. He climbed back into the truck and said he was thirsty, how about a drink?

Viejo clutched his throat and lolled his tongue, panting. "But I got no money."

"It's on me," Tre said, studying the side-view mirror, bending the rear-view to show him any tails. Nothing but parked cars.

"Órale!" Viejo started the engine. "I owe you one."

Now, that Viejo in the cowboy hat parked his truck on the Negra's street and directed a big blue van to pull up beside it. Viejo kept hanging his hand out the window, tapping on the door. He wouldn't meet Tre's eyes.

Tre was leaning against the rotting stucco wall of the house, picking at a bald patch in the vague shape of a large heart, with valves. The Negra came up beside him, set a hand on his shoulder and another in his pocket, and the two slouched together as if two parts, light and dark, glued together but not mixed. They were always together when he wasn't working. The older Mexican and White women who were still superstitious said that she hexed him because the black people were witches or devils or at the very least not to be trusted. The old black ladies said Tre was the devil, and he'd only bring her heartache. The younger folks said that the sex must have been good and wild.

Tre and the Negra whispered their suspicions to each other when the driver and passenger left the van and came around to the back. The driver was tall and thin like an athlete, and muscular, unlike the crowd gathered around. The passenger was chubby as a baby with darkly-dyed mustache and eyebrows and very little hair, though what there was had been dyed dark too. He carried a bullhorn with him and he cycled through the settings before raising it to his lips.

"… and we've brought you these gifts as a sign of our dedication to you. All we ask is for the same dedication to us, to those who want to make your lives better."

The driver's back muscles taxed his blazer when he pulled open the rear doors of the van. He stepped aside. In the van, stacked to the ceiling, were shining new tennis shoes of all colors, their plastic and faux-leather patches gleaming, their laces white and tightly woven as sun-bleached fish bones. The Negra took a toothpick from her mouth and put it between Tre's teeth. He gnawed at the toothpick and watched. Briefly, he raised an eyebrow and looked over a shoulder at the Negra, who was shaking her head.

At first just the younger ones swarmed the van. Then the older folks waded into the crowd. Shoes were passed overhead hand-to-hand to the elderly loitering on the fringes.

Tre tossed the toothpick, smacked the Negra on the rump and strolled over. As soon as he did so, Viejo drove his truck away, leaving only dust for Tre to glare into. Tre didn't need to push anyone aside, the crowd did that for him, and at the rear of the van the driver grunted at him. The politico with the bullhorn went back to his long list of promises.

Tre breathed in the thick smell of rubber and exhaust from the van. He took up a shoe, tugged the tongue out, read its insides and to him the shoes smelled just as dirty though they were brand new. Size 10. Right foot. He handed the first shoe to a hooting boy with camo shorts hanging off his hipbones, the shorts cut from a found uniform. Tre took up another shoe, handed it off. Size 8. Right foot. Another one. Another.

They were all for the right foot. He looked back to the Negra, who was guiding an old man wearing a pair of right-footed shoes, beaming, across the dirt yard.

The driver looked from Tre to the politico, who asked if his muscles were just for show. The politico turned off the bullhorn long enough to tell Tre, "Get out of here, huh? Don't make trouble."

Then he raised the bullhorn to his full pink lips and said, "The right shoe, from the right candidate, eh? Vote for me, and you'll get the rest. New shoes to walk into your new life."

Tre struggled to back out of the crowd of children and teenagers pushing harder for their sneakers, the pile now just a few scattered basketball shoes in the van, tongues lolling, misshapen from bearing the earlier weight of the rest.

When he got back to the wall where the Negra was waiting, boys were beginning to fight over the last remaining shoes, the van's doors were slammed shut, and both men were back in the van, shouting the politico's name as they drove off. They stopped once at the end of the road, where Viejo waited in his truck. Something passed between the drivers' windows and the Viejo tilted his cowboy hat in thanks.

"You believe that?" Tre asked.

A group of boys and girls had gathered round an old man who was checking their shoe sizes with half a broken ruler.

The Negra said, "You don't?"

Twenty-Four

One night soon after the drive to the beach, Rudy woke from a dream of his family in a desert. The desert had not been barren. It had been full of trailers gleaming like bullets and there had been many other families there, families he already knew, and some he didn't. And they all took their water from the same well, and they brought it down from the mountains a day's ride away, where they created a stepped irrigation system that looked from far away like green steps for gods.

Cheeks sore from smiling, Rudy sat up from sleep and rubbed his puffy eyelids with the tips of his fingers, tracing the shape of the iris beneath. Coming into focus beyond the glass wall of the fish tank was someone who looked just like the Capitan. But it wasn't him. It couldn't have been. His hair was disheveled and his shirt untucked and he wore pajama bottoms. He wore slippers on his feet, nice, but still, slippers. Rudy stood and shuffled his feet forward, to keep from waking the others. The Capitan's double floated forward like he were the one in a fish tank. His face was bloated as if he'd been under the weight of its dim waters for some time.

"I don't sleep," he mouthed.

"Never?" Rudy asked.

"Never."

"Why not?" Rudy could think of nothing but practical causes and solutions. "Don't you try tea, or liquor? Don't you try exercise?" After saying this, he felt foolish.

The Capitan, because that was indeed who this bloated ghost was, kept shaking his head. It was nearly impossible to hear through the glass. It was almost as difficult, for those of us hired to clean that dark warehouse at night, to read on their lips the words each man was trying to say.

"Come inside and talk," Rudy said.

"I can't."

Rudy looked at José, who lay face down on the couch, arms at his sides like a man shot dead, snoring. Maggie slept slumped in the chair with her legs sprawled, one pump on the ground, the other hanging from a toe. The room was filled with the usual blend of José's flatulence, the dusty smell of the professor's books, and the lemony-talc perfume that Maggie's Colonel preferred. Rudy noticed now that the Capitan had brought no new books. Though it was strange for this to trouble him, Rudy sensed that the Capitan was exhausted, stretched on a rack all his own. And it did trouble him. Somehow, the health of his captor had become intertwined with the health of his captive family. He pointed to the stacks of books on the desk and up against the glass walls on the floor.

"It's okay," Rudy said. "I have plenty. Everything's fine."

The Capitan didn't seem to notice the gesture. He was staring intently into Rudy's brown eyes with his own hazel—no longer like anything fancy, but gangrenous and sewn through with red threads.

"Your friend, the chili cook," the Capitan said.

"That was just something he did. What about him?"

"It was sloppy. It wasn't meant to be."

The Capitan said some more things, but either the glass was too thick or his voice was too soft or Rudy's ears were ringing too loudly for him to hear it. He couldn't read the Capitan's lips anymore. His eyesight was blurry like when he read without his glasses. Soon the Capitan receded into the dark, submerging, further and further from the surface, and Rudy told himself to hope, to hope like his daughter used hope, but for the exact opposite of outcomes for which she would use hers. Rudy hoped that the Capitan had never been there at all.

Twenty-Five

The girl behind the fancy department store counter smiled at Tre, frowned at his big friend Junior, and leaned her elbows onto the glass. Her heat fogged there. She wielded her false eyelashes like fans, and inside her low-cut yellow blouse her breasts looked battened against floating off, but just barely. In Tre's periphery, shoppers sped by the big display window. Junior walked off. Tre took note of a leather jacket Junior pulled off the rack, shiny, sleek, couldn't hardly tell the difference between the plain and the bullet proof. Junior said, "That could come in handy."

Maybe Tre would find something for himself today, too. But for now: "I need shoes."

"For a lady friend?" There went those fans again. He rubbed his own eye. It itched every time she winked. Maybe it was her perfume. She'd likely showered in Chanel numbers five through fifty.

"No. I need a hundred pair, all different sizes. Tennis shoes."

"No lady? Good to know. What sizes?"

"Whatever you got."

She licked her lips and popped some blue gum he hadn't noticed before. He'd thought it was her tongue she kept pressed beneath her bottom lip. "Cash or credit?"

His pocket was tight around it. Cash.

She said, "We talking a lot of numbers, aren't you gonna ask me for mine?"

Junior came back to the counter with the jacket, his silver chains and bracelets making music. "This too."

"Any chance you sell just the left ones?" Tre was asking.

She popped her gum. "Did you hear what I said?"

"Never mind. They should match anyway, right?" Tre asked himself.

She said "Whatevers," and went back to clacking the register with long red nails.

"Oh." Tre almost stopped her hand by touching the back of it, thought better, and flushed when she leered. "The jacket too."

"Thanks, dog, I owe you." Junior socked him on the shoulder, and with a quick glance at the gift, but looking mainly at the girl, said, "You a better man than me."

Twenty-Six

Rudy's wife didn't run out to greet him like we thought she would. Except for the constant buzz overhead from the helicopters, the air was still in a way it rarely was in our neighborhood. There were no children in the street. The front door was locked, and Rudy didn't have anything on him because he'd had to turn it all in at the jail, where the desk clerk had lost his box. That's what they'd said. We all knew that somewhere a soldier was wearing one of his nicest argyle sweaters to the café.

Rudy watched the military jeep furrow through its own dust and turn the corner. He must have wondered if they'd only be back to pick him up in a few days, wearing deep ruts in the road as he'd heard they could do once they suspected you. He found the door locked. He jiggled the knob. He knocked but no one answered.

Around back, in the alley, there was a pair of chanclas in the dirt beside his wall. They looked like they belonged to a giant, and he crouched down to study them with his crooked nose scrunched under his glasses, picked up a stick and used it to turn one chancla over. A leather chancla with a woven thong. Deep bowls where the balls of the feet would go. Eventually his curiosity got the better of him and he threaded the stick through the thongs and picked them up, leaned the stick over his shoulder. Then he climbed the fence.

When he neared the patio he froze in the dark shade of the avocado tree. Eight women lounged beneath all the hanging plants over the patio, trading stories about each of their failed or successful romances, and they had a game going of alternating stories so that after each they all would call out in one voice: frying pan, fire. He smiled at that. Then the smile twisted down into slack-mouthed real- ization.

If all these women were here, the only reason he could think of was that his family had been jailed too, and this pack of biddies had seized his property in their absence. It was, after all, one of the nicer lots in the neighborhood.

He strode out from beneath the tree with the stick held across his body, the chanclas flapping together at its tip like a foul-smelling morningstar.

Sally lumbered up onto those yellowed feet. "Why've you got my sandals?"

"What are you doing on my property?"

"Mr. Sellers?" Sally wound her way through the women, ducking her head to avoid the hanging plants. She took the stick from him and dropped her chanclas to the floor. Stepped into them. "You're so skinny." Conjured into her hand, with the speed and flourish of a magician, was a churro. "Eat something." Then he noticed the food, the baked goods, each deflated woman with a matching stale pastry in hand.

Rudy was staring unintentionally at Sally's withered cleavage and bright red skin when she embraced him. She was hot, and her armpits sweaty on his shoulders, and her dress a rough material like dust covers—her musty embrace reminded him of hiding with a flashlight and a book under his bed as a little boy, when he was scared. All the women stood then, shrieked with pleasure, and surrounded him, pinching his ribs and hopping around him with wide eyes and heads tilted quizzically. He was looking through them, trying to see answers inside everything now. "What are you all doing here?"

"We came to speak with your wife," Sally said.

"She's here?" Now he hugged back. "They're still here? They're okay?"

They all shrugged. Around the neighborhood words were spoken of his family, but never that one little word: okay.

"Well, where is she?" Rudy asked.

Sally hefted a thumb over her shoulder. "In the bathroom."

"So she'll be out any minute." Rudy clapped his hands together and smiled. "Good. I hope you don't mind excusing us."

Sally placed a wide hand on his shoulder. "Not using the toilet."

"What?" Rudy's hands hadn't yet moved since their clap.

"Not using it. Just in the bathroom. She hasn't left since you were arrested."

"Oh dear," Rudy said, working his hands into each other now. He ushered them through the back door, which was unlocked, and out the front. Then he went alone out onto the patio and stood beneath the bathroom window. Careful not to land in any of the pastries strewn around the patio, he hopped once or twice to see his wife.

"Leti. Leti, wake up."

"Rudy? Is that you? Hold on."

He heard her drop the toilet seat. Heard her grunt. He asked her what on earth she was doing and then her face was in the window— standing on the toilet, apparently. She had a wide new chin, right beneath the old one. Her jowls were luscious extensions of the old borders of her slim face, so that she seemed half-emerged from a puddle of peach colored paint.

"How long," he said.

"Stop studying me and give me a kiss." The window framed her beaming face like a painting by Botero.

He hopped once and kissed her cheek through the window. He tried again for the lips and he missed. "Come out of there now," he said. "I missed you."

"I'd love to," she said. "I've missed you so much."

He blushed, lowered his head. He was never one to let a person see him under the influence of emotion, even his wife.

She went on, "But I can't. I swore I wouldn't. When I leave this bathroom it's because we're leaving this country."

"Don't be melodramatic," he said. "Where's Tre?"

"How should I know?"

"Nora?"

"Classes, of course. She's your daughter."

"Isn't there anything I can do to get you out of there? There must be something."

"Bring me my boy. You have your daughter. Bring me Rudy Three."

"Why are you being this way?"

"Look at you. Why? You just got out of a jail that's known for murdering at worst and torturing at best. You and your daughter don't even flinch. Bring me my boy. He has a heart."

"You don't mean that."

"You say I'm melodramatic. Don't be academic. I mean it. I'm saying it, aren't I?"

He sighed and his shoulders drooped and he lowered his head. He could feel her breathing down on him and he limped to the back door.

She said, "What's wrong with you?"

He didn't say anything for a while, and then he said, "They gave me their best treatment, no?" He laughed lamely. Shrugged. "The worst, they gave to my friends."

"Let me hold you," she said.

He smiled, nodded. Waved her to him as if he could slide her through the window to his arms with only a gesture.

She shook her head no. "Come on," she said. "I'll open the door but only for you."

Twenty-Seven

One night with no stars, the neighborhood dogs grey ghosts sniffing alley puddles, four teenagers in raggedy camouflage clothes and armed with machetes and guns stampeded the home of the Negra. There were screams and the wind whipping the curtains seemed to come from the Negra, she shouted so loud.

Three of the adolescent guerillas dragged Tre from his home. The fourth staggered out with a crotch dripping darkness and a bloody pile of mess in his hands. For a long time it would be said that the Negra bewitched him when he'd tried to mount her, but really she'd just cut his manhood off with a steak knife. Either way someone knocked her out and she never came outside to watch what happened next.

The guerillas shouted in Spanish and English that Tre had betrayed his own people. They said: where did those shoes come from? From the politico. When a man said Tre had done nothing wrong, that he'd bought the shoes for them with his own money because what the politico had given them had been useless, one of the guerillas shot him. In the blast's echo he crumpled into the barren flowerbed and lay his head on the piled garden hose.

No one said anything after that. We all swayed side to side in the dark, trying to see over each other's shoulders while the three guerillas beat Tre about the eyes with the butts of their rifles.

His brow was a gorilla's, his eyelids shiny and swollen shut. His cheek was a ripe plum slit by sun. They hogtied him and swung him one two three through the air, into the bed of a pickup truck made almost entirely of old packing crates and shopping carts. Not a minute later they returned, slid to a stop in front of the house again, and the passenger got out this time with no weapon. He led the wounded one they'd forgotten from the house. The wounded one, as he passed each of the neighbors, held up his hand and showed the old ladies what was there, or not, begging them to fix him and calling them abuelita. The women kept dark hard faces and did not cry.

Spilling out of the house were the pages from Tre's sketchbook. Tissued on the wet dirt. Glued to the cement by muddy boot prints. They were all sketches of the Negra. Overly flattering, not nearly accurate, but good. The way someone remembers a lover they've not seen since youth and will never see again, an expectant kink in her cheek on the verge of becoming a smile. None of us could help it— from then on we all saw her how Tre saw her.

Just the day before that it was so hot we all sat outside—Tre and la Negra too—in the shade of our houses, watching the sunlight make waves above the street. We saw the two boys that always helped Tre hide his bike when he came back from working. The two boys, tall and short, had been playing some game of one-upmanship where they spat insults at each other in succession. Another boy had been playing too, but he got his feelings hurt and ran home crying, noodle arms at his side. The tall boy, Dale, was the better at the game. Ricardo had been growing red streaks across his face, redder than Tre's bike even. No one could hear what Ricardo finally said, though he said it loud, but he'd finally beat Dale and they got into a fist fight, twirling around like dancers, then wrestling on the hard-packed dirt road that runs alongside the cane. Tre had unleaned himself from his spot against the stucco where he liked to pick it away, said boys would be boys, smiling, and pinched the Negra's bottom on his way inside.

Early in the morning, before the boys played their game, an old man who takes his walks before the dogs wake up and likes to clap his floppy-soled shoes at the strutting chickens, saw a man get in a nice car at the end of the alley. It drove off in dust clouds thick like brown beans boiling over. Standing there in the street with a fist full of candy and a fist full of coins was the tall one named Dale.

And we all knew what he'd done.

Because the day before that, we'd seen one of the politico's goons skulking around the hood, a hulk smiling a craggy smile and trying to talk to kids. When fathers or mothers yelled at him to go away, he only adjusted the bright tie around his veined neck and turned a corner, searched another block. He'd been the driver when the politico had delivered the shoes.

It all made sense because the afternoon before that, when Tre had come home from work and Dale and Ricardo had come home to meet him, Tre told the younger Ricardo to put the bike away. Dale slouched his long figure over to a stack of old coke bottles and kicked them into the wall. Tre told him to clean them up. Told him he was almost a man, and had to act like one. Told him to learn responsibility, and that putting the bike away was a job for a boy, and tantrums for babies. Ricardo said Dale stomped off into the cane, and it was a real quiet night so we could hear Dale crying among the canes rattling with wind.

Only the day before that Tre had come with a truckload of tennis shoes, and everyone on his block got a pair. After we had all gotten our shoes and thanked Tre, praised him, taken him more dinner than one man could eat, some started in gossiping, saying: See how Tre smiled? So big? Could see his rotten teeth in the back? The professor would be sad to see his son smiling so. That smile can only be the smile of a dead man. Still, when we'd finished wearing those shoes for the day we put them in the cardboard boxes that we kept slid under our beds.

Now that Tre was gone, we said how good he was to us and how awful it was what had happened to him. Then we talked about what the Negra had done to that one's manhood, and we laughed with our heads tilted too far back, so you knew that really we were sad.

Occasionally one of us would quit wondering, quit whittling, take a cigarette off of our lips, and ask, who'll tell la Negra about Tre when she comes to?

But no one had an answer and the frogs only sounded that much louder, and the cockroaches scuttled up and down the walls. We crushed them with our heels, the old men saying ha!, but none of them meant it.

Twenty-Eight

Leticia shouted loud enough for all of us to hear. Inside, Rudy was trying his hardest to drag her from the bathroom. But Rudy was less muscle than he was bone, and Leticia, due to the frequent visits from the women and their pastries passed through the window, was swollen. Rudy, ignorant of the frequency and the quantity of the pastries, said that he was worried she was suffering some sort of edema.

"At the very least, you must be retaining water. Are you crying? Perhaps you're not letting yourself grieve."

He had her by the ankles and she gripped the pipes beneath the sink, anchored firmly to the wall. No matter how hard Rudy pulled, he couldn't even raise her belly into the air.

She hauled a knee up, donkey-kicked hard, and Rudy barely dodged a heel.

"That's it," he said. "I'll leave you in there. I'll study you. Relegate yourself to a disorder, if that's what you want." He left and shut the door.

"What I want is my boy. What I want is for us all to leave this place."

Rudy leaned his forehead against the door, reading the titles of the books that Nora kept stacked outside the bathroom. They were blurry and the words added up to one long title that was practically a book itself. He put his glasses on, as he always did when there was something difficult to deal with. He'd stopped reading much at all since he learned that his son was no longer staying gone of his own will. Word traveled faster from mouth to ear, he thought, than it ever did on paper.

"I don't know what to do," he said, his lips brushing the door. All of the windows were open. It was colder locked outside the bathroom than it must have been locked within. The teenagers and small children, that had heard the commotion, sat or hung on the branches of the avocado tree outside, chittering. Telling each other loudly to be quiet. He'd ceased allowing the neighborhood women to stay out on the patio since they'd spread the word of his son to his wife before he'd even learned it.

His wife didn't cry like any other woman he'd known. Not like his mother, the Puta, who cried endless torrents and seemed to cry all the moisture out of her face and body—at least that's what he'd heard. No, Leticia cried silently, gulping big breaths between sobs that racked her body but made no sound save the breathing. He could imagine her in the bathroom doing that now. When he closed his eyes, he saw her still.

"I've done what I could," he said. "You don't know what I've traded." He slapped the door, turned his crooked nose on the children in the windows, and they scattered. "I won't speak to that Capitan again. Not one word. And you. You know me. You think I've not thought this through?" Slapping his head, he whispered, "My brain is smooth from it."

She'd gone silent. Then, "Don't do that." Her voice rang hollow and distant against the tile. "Don't be poetic."

He pushed his glasses back up to the bridge of his nose. "I'm just being honest." He often squeezed his nose now, as if he could force it straight again.

She whispered something.

"What?" he said.

She whispered it again. A few times, before she said it loud enough for him to hear. "You call the Capitan," she said flatly. "Or you ask your daughter to."

Rudy stood outside of his daughter's bedroom door but he couldn't bring himself to knock. He couldn't be indebted to her, so in love with that Capitan that she would trade her family. Even the word trade enraged him for its reminder of his own underhanded bartering of his friend's life. And his wife, as long as they were stuck in this place she was no wife to him at all.

The house was cold, colder than any weather could make it. His hand hovered near his daughter's door, which he had once used to let himself into the breezy room sometimes just to look at her, just to see her smile from the corner where she read beneath the window. The doorknob was cold too.

So he found another way. He started by telling his daughter that she could not go to class anymore. Simple enough. But she was his daughter and without analyses, simply by twisting her hair round the pencil in her hand, she could discern that it was not for her safety alone that she was to stay in the house.

The house was always dark now—they always looked upon each other as shadows. She stood at the end of the hall. He sat in his chair looking over the bills, tearing up the electricity and the water because he had no job and no way to pay for those things. Besides, others used candles, older men than he toted buckets to the wells.

"Do you hear me?" she yelled down the hall when he had work to do.

He had never spent so much time in the house. He raised a letter, one of many risky letters reaching out to friends abroad, closer to the candle. Squinting down his nose at the flickering flame, he said: "There seems to be a draft in this house."

When the phone began to ring regularly late at night, he jumped eagerly out of his lonely bed thinking it must be the Capitan. Then, in a guilty fury over his excitement, he pounded on Nora's door. He listened outside the door, tortured by indecision. What good was leaving if he left his pride behind? What good was staying if he lost his family in the process?

Nora was whispering in there. He remembered love whispers. Nora and the Capitan wouldn't spend much longer apart.

Rudy spidered his fingers along the cord, through the hall, to the living room, where he yanked it from the wall. As he was heading back to bed, she came and stood in the hall once more. The house was so drafty, the light so blue and quivering, and her so thin and her nightgown so ephemeral, that she appeared to be held to this house only by the weight of that large black phone in her hand. She stood lopsided, with the phone digging into a thigh.

"He's dangerous," Rudy said.

"To whom?" she asked. "You?" She bit her lip. Rudy knew she regretted saying it instantly.

"No," he shook his head. She had disappointed him, and he knew she wanted so badly for him to yell at her now. He wanted so badly to yell too. Instead he said, "To us, no?"

She shook her head, grasping for something indisputable. "You looked left. You're lying." She wasn't sure if this was true, and rather than face him anymore she turned and floated around the corner to her room.

The door shut behind her.

His hand tugged up suddenly, until he released the phone cord.

It dragged along the floor and snapped against the wall and burned the bottom of the door when it snaked in after her.

Twenty-Nine

At night, through the living room window, we could see the candlelight flickering. Rudy kept watch in his chair beside that candle, often thinking of his daughter at a younger age. Keeping watch for what, he wasn't sure. These fears, of nothing in particular, were the most difficult to dispel.

In the past, he and Nora had made weekly trips to the libraries, a circuitous trek through many neighborhoods poor and well off, to purchase used books off tables set up outside the buildings. At the poor libraries, Rudy and Nora purchased the classics: a quarter for Crusoe with no dust jacket, a dollar for a coffee stained collection of Twain. She'd make a game of the hunt, running around the tables to be the first to spot the book that would make her father set his glasses high on his nose and look down, at her showing him all her tiny white teeth. Then she'd laugh and run around the tables some more. At the libraries in the nicer neighborhoods, they'd find the newest books, the prizewinners and the best-sellers, out of England, or Latin America, the occasional exile from California, American expats riding the second, bigger wave to Spain. They'd look through their new books on a park bench and thumb the bindings. They'd trade books and do the same again.

Now, the Capitan would come for her. How could he not? Here was a young woman who loved him, kept hostage from love by her own father, hoping that, by keeping her away like this, he would find the son who had almost killed him.

But this, his daughter's love for this Captain who'd committed acts of unspeakable malice, this hurt more than any bullet ever could have. A bullet would have been instant, would have cauterized the vacuum even as it ripped the vacuum open. But there was no bullet, and there was a vacuum in Rudy's gut now, a vacuum that felt the size of a cavern, a vacuum big enough to hold his wife, his son, his daughter's failing love, his murdered friends, and his hatred for his enemies whom he did not know how to recognize. He sat in the fading candlelight, a hunched figure in the yellow glow.

We all knew what was happening to him, because it happened to all of us eventually. Having that tender womb in which we kept things, turned them over, asked them to grow so we might understand; it only meant more hurt. He was teaching himself in that chair, each night, waiting for his confrontation with the Capitan, trying to cauterize that womb himself, to fill it with stones so that in a flood of emotions he'd not be carried away, but instead be anchored to the bottom, running his fingers over the armrests of a chair, hoping for nothing but sleep.

Until a wayward stone hit the window at the front of the house, burst through the glass and wound spinning down in a glittering bed of light at his feet.

See, Sally's teenage boy who had been out late with a rich girl he wasn't allowed to see—the poor are prejudiced of the rich just as violently as the rich are of the poor—was waddling home bowlegged and nearly asleep to boot.

His elephantine feet, inherited from Sally, ironically enough earned him a certain reputation with the ladies, and gave him a plodding gait even when not oversexed as he was now. A sleek car the color of butter even in the dark of night shot round a corner, and the boy started to one side of the road, then the other, then was caught in the narrowing beams of the headlights when suddenly the car swung wide of him and a blur of a blond man with white teeth shot by cursing and stopped maybe ten feet away.

The boy looked around. He had Sally's heavy bottom lip and slow-lidded eyes.

The town was asleep.

He didn't want trouble so he ran.

He had to stop several times, because of a cramped groin. And several more times he stretched his legs against the ramshackle fence posts along the road. By the time he got home, his groin was hurting worse than before, and he muttered curses at the rich girls and their whorish ways and blamed their spoiled natures for their insatiable appetite. That was no excuse for being late, though, not an excuse to give his mother.

Sally, who'd been waiting up, opened the front door, and he blurted that a rich man in a butter car hit him coming round the corner, and he'd managed to get away before the rich man tried to disappear him. Sally, heavy fists against the doorframe, ducked beneath the transom. Her sunburned skin looked for once milky, thanks to the moonlight, but the boy flinched when she slammed her palm against the door.

The boy faked a few sobs, and hobbled back a few steps.

"Are you hurt?" she asked.

He nodded.

Sally said, "Go inside and tell your brother to run to Rudy's."

When the boy walked inside Sally watched him swing a heel forward, settle it, then swing the other around into place. That bastard the Capitan, she must have been thinking. "No one rides down my sweet little boy!"

The older boy fought to keep a stern face after that dirty innuendo. But her littlest boy, the one they sent, was a chunky moron inclined toward recklessness, and he ran a collision course through the night and its soft flowerbeds and prop-like fences, often not even bothering to jump.

When he got outside Rudy's house, he took up a handful of stones to toss at the glass like his brother had told him but, misremembering the instructions, instead of choosing stones the size of his pinky to the first knuckle, he chose stones from the rocky asphalt and dirt in the street that were the length and width from his pinky-tip to his wrist. The first one he let go late and it bounced once at his feet in shadow. The second one he threw clear of the house and a rooster squawked in the alley.

He crouched down to pick up a new one, and considered for quite some time.

Teeth clamped bottom lip in concentration. Eyes narrowed into slits.

The third stone, its arc and speed showing marked improvement, burst through Rudy's window.

Rudy stood in the front doorway of his home wearing an old purple bath-robe of Leticia's, staring out at the dark simple yard of dead grass and dying plants. He passed his eyes left to right once and again before he noticed the small round boy waving from only a few feet away, at which point the boy dropped a pile of stones at his feet and dusted the belly of his shirt, in which he'd been holding them.

"Mama told my brother to tell me to tell you."

"To tell me what?"

The boy shrugged.

"Who's your mama, then?"

"I can't tell strangers that. What if you're a bad guy?"

"But," Rudy pleaded, "I'm not a bad guy."

The boy shook his head no. Rudy shook his head no, to be sure. The boy shook his head no, this time with force. And what force. No one could have made that kid budge. His tenacity was equal parts determination and simple-mindedness, traits the professor thought equaled success more times than not, and the most successful person at doing only what they wished, well, that was Sally. That meant she had seen or heard word that the Capitan was in the neighborhood. Rudy tied the belt of Leticia's bathrobe tight and shut the door.

The boy grinned and kicked a stone out into the street. He raised his arms to cheer himself. He looked around the empty street, looked up at the moon. Then he stuffed his hands in his pockets and walked off, trying to memorize exactly what had happened so he could recount the story for us as best he could, and laugh dumbly, proudly, like how we would all encourage the pobrecito to do.

Rudy found the Capitan assisting Nora as she climbed out the window. His steps had been light in the dead grass of the back yard, and both the Capitan and Nora were smiling so wide their eyes nearly closed. Rudy waited until Nora was out of the window and, hand in hand, they both turned to face him.

"You're not taking her until you promise to help find our son and get us out of here."

Nora said, "You'd trade a daughter?"

Rudy stepped forward, the belt of the bathrobe wrapped twice around him still hung slack past the knot. "You want to go, go."

The Capitan stepped forward, let go Nora's hand though she left it lifted behind him a while. "I'm sorry."

"Are you?"

"I'll give her a life you can't give her."

"And whose fault is that?"

By now, the word of what would happen had passed from house to house, and slowly our teenagers were creeping along the walls, and even quicker the mothers were pouring into the backyard, over the fence, through the unlocked front door. We'd formed a line from the bathroom window in the patio, inside of which Leticia's face could be seen, all the way out under the avocado tree and to the back of the house where Rudy stood before the Capitan, and Nora stood behind them both shooing us away.

"Certain times we do what we have to," the Capitan said.

Rudy shook his head and asked again, "Whose fault is it?"

"There is a standard operating procedure—"

"There's a standard for this?" Rudy asked. "What is it? What is the procedure?" He gathered breath into his chest when the Capitan began to answer, and everyone was silent. Rudy looked like he would burst, he took so much air in, but when the Capitan didn't answer after all, Rudy let the air out in a whisper, "Nobody knows anything about anything anymore."

The words he said were said again and again down the line of women in Spanish then English, English then Spanish, until finally Sally, the last woman, whispered in through the window of the bathroom, inside of which Leticia gathered her sleeping gown about herself and sighed against a fogging tile on the wall.

Rudy and the Capitan didn't speak for a while. The grass crunched under the Capitan's feet, where he alternated his weight like an unchallenged fighter. He reached back for Nora's hand.

"My son is missing," Rudy said.

The Capitan must have remembered not out of malice, but habit, that he held the upper hand; remembered too that he had an audience, and struck a proud posture.

Rudy noticed. "Why did you speak to me that way that night?"

The Capitan swept a stiff arm around at the teens on the wall and the women in the yard. "He's under enormous stress."

"Not you?" Rudy asked.

"Quiet." The Capitan's teeth were clenched. His jaw dimpled deep high up near his cheek.

"Why did you confess to me?"

"I have nothing to confess. And you couldn't hear a thing through that glass."

"I didn't have to hear your voice to know what you were saying."

"I'm taking Nora with me."

All the while the women kept chattering back the words that each man said so that there was never a quiet moment and it made both men more skittish. Both men looked confused. But then the noise dropped out. The men looked around, forgot themselves and their confrontation with each other. A wide shadow stretched across the lawn and when Leticia emerged from the dark beneath the avocado tree she seemed birthed from it, was shaped like an avocado herself. A few of the boys on the wall snickered.

Leticia was holding her belly like the unaccustomed weight it was. She jammed a flat palm against her lower back. "You can have her when you've found our son."

The Capitan let Nora go. He scanned the crowd, the family, smiled at Nora. He stepped over to Rudy, leaned in and whispered, "Tell Nora everything you know, yeah?"

"She won't concern herself with anything I have to say."

"Make her, then. You're the man of the house, no?"

Rudy stood taller at that.

The Capitan went on. "Tell her what you know. Maybe she won't even want to stay with me. Maybe she'll make this easier for all of us."

Thirty

In the back of the pickup truck the air was so thick with dust that Tre gummed it in his sleep. He woke, nostrils deep tunnels snaked into clay. He kept his eyes shut because when he tried even a little to open them the dust ran quick and thick as sand into what fissures he could make.

Beside him, someone whimpered. Cried. Tre shook his head and banged it against the soft planks that held them above the humming chassis, near enough to feel the steel twist the air around and around. He shook loose enough dust to see the Guerilla beside him, crotch and belly and thighs all soaked in blood. The guerilla's crotch was a dark red crease the man couldn't bear to look at; he kept begging Tre—a sound that only now Tre realized he'd been hearing even in the smothering unconsciousness—to look at it, to tell him was it okay.

"It's not," Tre said.

The guerilla asked God for help and clenched his eyes, clenched his jaw, then all at once snapped his head down to see the gaping wound that looked like a woman's parts run through. He whimpered long and low.

Tre looked away. In the grime of the rear window the three guerillas sat nearly atop one another, laughing at something with the radio turned loud.

The wounded one said, "Your bitch did this."

Tre tried to kick him but only thrashed against his plastic bindings. "Undo these. Undo these and I'll help."

"Help how?"

"Do we have far to go?"

"Fuck you. I ain't telling you that shit."

"If we do, you're dead."

The guerilla shut his eyes again. When he opened them, tears welled up into the mud along their rims, and the eyeballs themselves were splotched red. Tre couldn't look at his face anymore. The guerilla's boot-toe was shredded to the steel. They had a long way to go. Probably they'd already come a long way.

Rising up around them were concrete walls covered in green. Now and then they'd pass through tunnels, or beneath overpasses, and things were bright, then black; bright, black; the sound of the tires squelching through water meant they were traveling one of the many riverbeds either to or away from the ocean. They were somewhere in that place called the Jungle. In the winters, the guerillas like ants swarmed out of their flooded homes in the concrete cracks and ransacked the locals; in the summer heat like this, they dwelt near the water with the poor ones and the drugged ones and the crazy ones too.

The green walls quaked in the hot wind, the overgrowth wilting so low at times that Tre could smell the green air and think of making love to his Negra in the backyard with the cane shimmying in the wind and the little boys and girls hooting as they hopped the fence to watch, running when the Negra threw a sandal, a rock.

The guerilla was crying outright now, but quietly. The sound of the jeep's radio seemed to shrink from the light, growing louder in the dark recesses beneath streets and freeways, dispersing each time the pickup burst back out into the day.

One of the guerillas leaned out the passenger window, looked at his comrade, shook his head.

The wounded one cried from the bed for his help.

Inside the cab, the passenger leaned toward the dash and the music got louder.

The next time they passed into the dark, Tre scooted his body down the bowing planks. When they crossed back into the daylight, traffic rushed above them on the 405 Freeway. Anymore, the freeway functioned like a railroad tracks. The people who lived between its stops generally stayed put, and the ones who lived at its stops in L.A. or the resort towns of Playas, passed only from one to the other. A fence ran along the side and a large banner read THIS IS WHAT HAPPENS TO JOURNALISTS in bold red letters. A hung body turned in the wind beneath it.

The guerilla's eyes were wide, glazed now, and he was mouthing something. Tre barely heard it for the music and the rattling of the ramshackle truck bed.

"You're going now?" the guerilla asked.

Tre said, "Yeah. I am."

The guerilla nodded, but by the way he tucked his chin to his chest Tre knew he was sad to die alone, and didn't want Tre to go. Tre noticed how smooth his pale face was, how young and, with the baggy fatigues plastered to his torso and thighs by the blood, how small.

Tre wormed his way to the edge of the bed and when they passed again into total darkness he shut his eyes though he told himself he didn't need to, and he rolled himself off. The feeling was of having everything solid tugged out from under and that feeling was so strong that solid became a suddenly strange and frightening thing. Solid. Hard. It was the only thing. When he landed first on one shoulder bound back, the bindings snapped, his ear aflame, an elbow gone electric, the other ear burned, lips kissed pavement, a gap opened where there'd once been a tooth, teeth where there'd been tongue, and pumping through him almost as hot as the blood in his mouth was the sense that hard were the only things he knew anymore.

Thirty-One

It was a standoff. The daughter read day and night and the father not at all. Nora found new and ingenious ways to keep the reading going twenty-four hours a day, and Rudy knew ways to plug his ears or songs to hum or records to play on the old Victrola, the only heirloom his family hadn't yet pawned. It had resided in Rudy I's bookstore beneath a stack of books on birdwatching and jazz, one of which was the bird book Rudy had read while imprisoned by the Capitan. Now Rudy wouldn't even read that, and Nora read out loud the books that made him cringe most, books that she knew he'd loved and now made him sweat. One night, he scooped the melted wax of his candle with a spoon, thumbed it into two small bullets, and stuck them into his ears.

When Nora read, she always kept a tape recorder on hand, so that if she needed a break she could rewind, press play, and let the recorder play her voice at full volume. She didn't like to do this often, though, because, one, she didn't like the way her voice sounded, quavering and raw, and low for a young lady's, and two, the effect on her father was not the same. Somehow he knew when the voice was a recording, not his actual daughter but a ghost of his daughter, and he snored, finally at peace in his chair with a piece of cane in one hand and a whittling knife in the other. Really, he preferred the recordings. He smiled about having the recordings to listen to after his daughter's inevitable exit from the house, the family, and they set him at ease because they weren't the live projection of his daughter's spite.

Nora had seen him fall asleep with the whittling blade in hand more than once, and more than once in his sleep he had cut himself deeply, trying to whittle his thumb into something he never seemed to remember when he woke, suddenly, hissing at the pain and kissing the blood, and so she was too frightened to play the recordings anymore, and he ceased sleeping, and then she lost her voice from reading aloud, and both of them withered in the dark while the mother grew fatter on pastries in the bright light of the oil lamps women brought her, and the house was quiet as it can only be when people who can speak won't.

So the girl left. Se fue. And maybe it was better that way.

Thirty-Two

There are different accounts of how far Tre was from home, when he staggered through the concrete riverbed holding his limp left arm against its aching socket. Different accounts, because not many people knew the routes of the guerillas' world. Different accounts, because the only people as brutal as the government were those guerillas. And so no account could be true, just truer.

The account that seemed truest to our ears said that Tre was someplace in North Playas, a long day's walk from home. He headed back the way they'd come, shambling over trash, around furniture and machinery stripped and tossed down the embankment. The whole sunken scene was a diorama of what happens to the world beneath a red, red sky. Looking for the quickest path up the embankment, he tried but skidded a few times down the smooth concrete. Once, bones crunched beneath Tre's tennis shoes, so he trudged on as well he could, loose arm swinging, and only looked back once. By then the rib cage was easily just the carcass of a game bird, the remnants of some holiday feast, if he wished.

When he'd begun his escape the pickup had disappeared from his head as easily as it had from his sight. But now the sound of its engine crawled over the expanse of concrete from so many directions he couldn't be sure where it was, only that it was near, and gaining ground not just by nearing but by swallowing all ideas of distance or retreat.

High above Tre, at the end of a rope, swayed the journalist's body—the tongue, black as shoe soles; the eyes, great white pearls. The body wasn't stripped, but the clothes were ripped in places fringed with dark blood. The rope creaked when the wind blew and behind Tre, in a dark alcove beneath the freeway, pigeons cooed and reminded him of the sounds his mamma used to make to help him sleep. Wings flapped and white feathers fell like a strange season of snow in this otherworld riverbed running a scar through the real one. Tre studied the wall behind the journalist to see how he'd been hung so high.

Tre asked himself, how would I have done it?

Not from the freeway.

From beneath it.

A rusty access ladder ran up the side of the wall, and he tested a rung by hanging from it with his good arm. Then he leaped at the highest rung he could reach, and, only when he'd gotten a knee up onto the lowest, began to climb. The injured arm hung like a scarf.

He buried his nose into his shoulder when he neared the journalist's body, but he lost his footing on the next step up and hung from one rung by the crook of his good arm. The wind forced the rotten smell on Tre, and spun the body so that he and it were face to face. He climbed, gagging.

For a moment, at the top of the ladder, he looked down on the journalist's parted hair, on the concrete three stories below, and Tre's head swam red as if the overpass were suddenly snatched away and he were teetering at the top of the sky. But then he found a way to tuck a shoe tight between a bar and the wall, and he found grip even in the slippery shit the pigeons left when they swapped, in a grey flurry, the alcove for the dusk.

Tre was missing now from the picture of the man spinning slowly on his rope, the picture that the guerillas must have seen from far below where their truck beetled over the concrete, the picture that should have been, but never was, in the papers. Maybe it was the air, warm and stagnant, maybe the creaking rope, but Tre always said that he could hear it—death. Could hear that the guerilla was dead in the bed of the pickup below, could hear that the hanged man had no life, could hear from this far that his Negra might be dead too. He wished more than anything for the pigeons to come back and to coo so loud he felt it rattle his chest, so he could hear nothing else. But the pickup went away. Night was the only thing that came. And Tre was alone with the floating man's moonlit form, and the creaking. That creaking rope.

Thirty-Three

Nora strolled through the Capitan's austere home with the quizzical eye of a botanist. She looked over the study, where a large wooden chair was tucked into a large desk and, though both were polished, neither looked used. She read significance into what there was to read on the bookshelf, a single shelf upon which were the only knick-knacks and mementos she would find in the house. Commendations. Certificates. Pins.

There were places for guests to sit, but the whole place impressed upon her that not much sitting took place. It was open, and there were clear lines of sight to nearly every door from nearly every spot in the room, and the whole place hummed with the momentum of an office instead of the tranquility and boredom of a home—especially her home, which had once smelled of food cooking in its kitchen, knowledge and dusty time on its shelves.

She took up a small pin, studied it under her sharp nose. It was tarnished, but filigreed in its center, a motto in Latin inscribed there.

The Capitan: a blur in her periphery. "My father's."

She nodded, turned it round: argento publico. But argento patris was more accurate. She was feeling everything about the house like every piece of her were as sensitive as the tip of a finger, which she now brushed over the spines of the few books in his small bookshelf. In one swipe, she'd touched them all.

"I guess I'm not as literary as you might like." He cleared his throat and she stopped classifying his home—her home now, was that possible?—and he came into focus, turning her by the shoulders and bringing in his high long face for a kiss.

"I don't want you to be." Standing face to face, they each had to lower their heads uncomfortably to rest them upon each other's shoulders.

"Used to be all at the office, the medals. There's some younger ones now that want my position. I have to keep my medals and pins here now just so the kids won't play dress up."

Nora smiled at his joke, but he didn't. "And the plane my father asked about?"

"I'll take care of that myself." The Capitan's eyes were recessed in his head and there were shadows and crevasses around them that hadn't been there when they'd first met.

"Good." She inhaled, about to say something else, then shook her head. "I can't stand this. You make me so flustered. You make me imprecise."

"What do you mean by that?" he said, smiling.

"I—" she began, but then pushed him away, laughing, and ran through the new house, nervous, excited, her laughter bright as the wooden floors that seemed to slip out from beneath her feet, stutter-stepping over carpets she did not know would be there, turning at corners with her arms out in case she met a wall or shut door. She had the sense that open doors were open just for her and closed doors closed for her to open them. She flung the bedroom door wide and dove into the bed. He was upon her when the doorbell rang.

"Who's that?" she asked. "Can't you send them away?"

He hung by an arm from the bed post, his body slack as a flag, his clothes more draped than usual, and her lips pinched because she saw all at once his deterioration. In her backyard, he'd been too symbolic of something to see truly. Her spirit seeped suddenly into the sheets that had been cool, but were already warm and staled by her presence in them.

"Don't worry." He ran a hand over his smooth hair. "It won't take long. It's just the neighbors coming to get to know you."

"And to go off and gossip about me when they get the chance."

"Gossip is what the poor people do."

"What does that mean?"

"It came out wrong. What I meant to say was you don't have to worry about that here. No one talks about anything. If there's no good to say, no one says anything. It makes for very quiet but very distinguished parties, and very boring."

She looked down at the dress she'd worn from home. It was a finely made thing of smooth silk and cotton, wispy at the neck, and the bottom layered in the style of a peasant dress. "Should I change?"

"Do you want to?"

"I don't know."

"Then maybe you should."

Thirty-Four

Tre woke in the alcove beneath the rumbling freeway. He was careful not to look at the body hanging bright and golden in the morning light, and climbed carefully down the rungs of the ladder, injured arm swinging but dull, throbbing at the shoulder, like all those taut strands of muscle bunched there were any moment going to bloom into something bright and pretty.

Eventually he found an access path, cement fault-lined by stunning green grass. The path wandered its way to the top of a tall slope, where the land dropped away from him into a lagging valley. He saw it rumpled and bunched like the green comforter his mother had kept on her bed when he was a child.

The trees, the grass, the ivy, the swaying palms grew wildly through ruins of houses, new wood slat ones, and old apartments as identical as prison cells. All the buildings overgrown, everything smelled and pulsed and flickered with life when the sunny wind rolled across their leafy backs. Beyond the brown grid of our hood, the Jungle must have looked to him at the same time hard-edged and mystic, buildings like shanks raised at the throbbing heart of a sun.

Somewhere to the west was the ocean but all he smelled was green and the seagulls, circling so high, called contentedly to each other like they'd never need to land.

Water hoses ran under his feet from the riverbed, duct taped together to run for hundreds of yards, into the old barrio he'd never seen, the one that'd been bought up long ago for rebuilding, for infrastructure, and in which squatters still lived their lives like there were no wrecking balls in slow swing, no cranes and dozers like beasts from a past nearly as overgrown as this one, the past he slouched to now using the good hand to tuck the loose hand of the wrecked arm into a pocket.

Once inside the barrio he felt more at ease—familiar sounds, children, radios, even pots and pans. The buildings, though overrun here by plant life, their soft stone edges crumbling, were vibrant. Barefoot children dangled legs out of windows and women with scraps of cardboard boxes scraped dust from doorways into the street.

Hoses on the floor branched from thick bunches like veins, snaked up walls into windows. Once, he passed a rusted trough filled with water and he drank from it. Near his forehead, a mosquito touched down inside a growing ring on the water. He drank until a pack of dirty dogs crowded around him and drank too, and he backed away scraping his tongue with a knuckle.

An old man laughed from the window above, the smoking pipe in his mouth made from a soda bottle. "It's their world, no?"

Thirty-Five

We all knew the servant class came from somewhere. Mostly, we looked down on them for taking the easy way out. Cleaning and prancing and dancing for dollars. In some way we were just jealous. Not Tre, though. That wasn't his style.

The distant flatbed truck inched down a long brown road and on one corner a mob of boys in shorts and dress-shirts watched it and waited. The boys had perfect posture and slick hair. They held serving napkins over their forearms and the skin on those arms like everyone else's here was a creamy bronze, a bronze filmed over by polish. They spoke so rapidly, and with so many words that Tre didn't know, that he thought it was a different language for a moment before it hit him that it was a thicker version of the slang in his neighborhood. Negra's.

A girl walking a little boy down the street could have been Negra, but lighter and whittled away here and there; the ribs, the rocky pelvis.

He smiled and she looked away.

"Wait, please."

"Qué you gots very necesario? Qué'yuda I gots?" She patted the kid on a pale shoulder blade, and he scrambled down the street calling out to friends. Some jumped out of shady spots. Some whined from unseen places that their parents would not let them play.

"Long Beach. I need a ride to the train station."

"Rolling Playas way, that hoopdie no va mas past the blue. But from here to there, no trouble."

She smiled at him, a smile that crinkled the skin stretched tight over her cheekbones and brow. She swept her golden hair to one side and showed a downy sideburn. She smiled wider, her eyes glinting, and showed him some spaces where teeth had been.

"Apurate," she said forcefully, "you roll." She wasn't pushing him off, just letting him know the truck was near. He hadn't heard its motor until now, and it was a loud one. It rattled and coughed the rich stink of leaded gasoline.

The truck had pulled up in front of the boys on the corner. The hood read Ocean Club of Las Playas. A man in a visor cap sat the driver seat. A man with a pistol sat shotgun. The boys were filing onto the back of the flatbed, and Tre couldn't imagine the trees breaking away anywhere down that shady brown road—what little light streamed through like a river of gold—but they must, and it must, because the truck was now turning round.

"Thanks," he called over a shoulder.

She was already half a block down, and she stopped with a bare dirty heel up. The truck was grumbling its way through a U-turn in the empty intersection and Tre cut to it before he could hear if she said anything. She had looked just like a version of his woman, a version of his own life lived by his own rules of living. The boys in the truck looked puzzled, and to him they must have looked just like her, dirty, ill, but so smooth skinned and subtly hued and properly placed features of face that they were small statues. When he reached out a hand a young one at the back took it. The exhaust was bitter on the back of Tre's tongue, hot in his chest. His injured arm tugged free of his pocket as he ran. When it began to swing, Tre grimacing, more boys decided to help him, made room, reached out.

His weight left him for a moment and then he was on the truck, just like the boys, gripping one of the ropes that railed the bed to keep from bouncing off. The small ones around him were smiling. Most of the older ones leaned their forearms on the truck's roof, staring ahead, backs rigid, heads bobbing silent agreement with each rut in the road.

Thirty-Six

The first surprise is not that she finds him talking to himself. The first surprise is the birds.

When Nora opened the front door she thought the cooing meant a pigeon had nested inside the chimney. This had happened once in her parents' house and her mother had been so scared of the disease the pigeons were blamed for spreading that Tre was made to poke and prod the chimney with a broom from below, drop buckets of hot water from the roof, and finally drop a rock through until all they found in the fireplace was the rock, and a smashed egg they thought looked just like freckled skin.

Nora didn't believe the birds spread disease at all. She thought it was all hearsay, a way for the people to blame sickness on something tangible because so much was out of their hands. But the cooing, when she shut the door on the cool street sounds, came loudly down the hall from her bedroom. It occurred to her she'd left a window open, and she sped across the hardwood floor raising her arms to shoo the birds.

But these birds were not going anywhere.

The silver cage sat on top of the bed and the Capitan with it, tapping at a delicate bar and cooing at the doves in return.

"What's this?" she asked.

"We'll release them," he said, only now looking up, so vulnerable, hiding behind the cage as if any moment he might return to whatever conversation he'd been having with the doves should the conversation with his girlfriend go downhill.

"Where'd they come from?"

"The bird-keeper will bring more. I've already paid her…"

"I mean origin. Where'd they come from? Colombia? The Pacific? They're not North American doves."

"They're not?" He studied them with a furrowed brow. "I thought…look, Nora, what does it matter if they're from outer space—I thought we'd release them at our wedding." Sweat shone on his forehead, divots deep there, and dark.

"I didn't mean—" She went to him quickly, and placed her hand on his cheek.

He smiled, but his eyes lingered on the cage. "You knew what it meant all along. You were just playing with me, weren't you?"

"Yes. Yes."

"You were just playing," he said. "I knew that."

The second surprise is that he's not talking to himself late at night anymore.

When she finds him, the Capitan is hanging in the hammock in the warm night's air, lighting one cigarette with another. The crickets are loud and the sound swells from a low drone to a piercing pitch. She always finds him like this. Her feet, bare, feel good on the cool cement of his patio.

As they'd felt good on the ceramic tile in the kitchen where she'd watched him shudder, the kitchen doors accordioned so that the outside and inside are one warm dark space.

And her feet had felt just as good treading down the hall.

Before that she was in the too-hot bed in the stuffy bedroom of corners and edges and precisely placed things that stand on a dresser and she doesn't yet know the room well enough to know what those things are. The simplest sound, the scrape of his match outside, had awakened her alone in that room. The room she returns to now, still afraid to ask and know what keeps him awake nights.

Thirty-Seven

The door to the Negra's house was made of corrugated steel, the hinges held by nail-pierced bottle caps. It creaked open and Rudy rolled the newspaper felted by age into a long narrow tube.

The Negra said, "We don't read the news, old man."

"No, I'm not selling this." He held out the newspaper, then hid it behind his back, remembering that sources of information were questionable no matter who you were. Especially a source like his, in an area like this. Inside the newspaper, the bold black writing had bled through the Capitan's handwritten note. "I'm looking for Rudy Three."

She slammed the door and it nearly bucked off its hinges. He knocked again. A moment later she opened the door, but this time she was holding a steak knife in her right hand and she'd pulled her hair back from her face, which was grim, as if she didn't want him to splatter into her hair when she cut him. Her face was slick in places from unhealed wounds, their grease coagulating into something between moss and scab. She jutted her chin, as if calling attention to the wounds. Not bashful, this one. Not vain.

"How you know his real name?" she asked.

"I know him." He stuffed the newspaper into his pants pocket.

She raised the steak knife. "Anyone that know him, know him as Tre."

Rudy removed his glasses, folded their arms in, and hung them from his shirt collar, open and flat, faded. Since his wife was locked in and his daughter had left, he'd not done the laundry properly once. He acknowledged himself for her, apologetically. "I'm his dad."

She stepped outside and looked down the quiet and empty block. It was a cool afternoon and it had been a hot, hot day, so the town was a rare soft calm, like we all were in a nap, and most of us were. The soft sunlight made the edges of the buildings yield, and the shadows through the trees fell like lace. She turned her eyes on him but didn't move her head. One dark eye regarded him like a stone from its tapered setting.

"You're lucky I didn't stab you on accident. Or on purpose. With no man here, it's only a matter of time before someone comes to take me or the place." She regarded him, more warmly now, a look that didn't seem to be aimed at him, but beyond. "You look like him," she said. "Just whiter, taller, and nicer. Maybe he has your eyes."

He smiled. "I'll take that. Do you know where he is?"

She shook her head. Became very interested in a dog curled up in the shadow of a palm's crown. "He got disappeared. A few days ago. Early morning. Late night. I don't know."

Rudy touched her elbow and she didn't pull away, but she locked her arm out like she'd practiced being stony for a while before he'd got there. Rudy wasn't good at these things, at emotional things. He knew he should apologize for her hurt, should feel his own, but he was too busy figuring out some way to reclaim his son from that foggy place between life and certain death, called disappearance. Then he was remembering his own arrest. Then the reasons for that arrest. Then he wondered if he was the reason behind all the reasons he'd told himself were at fault. Maybe reasoning was just a way to accumulate excuses for one decision made a long time ago.

"I'm sorry," he said, finally, dropping his hand from her arm. She looked at him like she'd forgotten he was there. "Who was it?"

"Guerillas."

"Why?"

"I don't know. Maybe something to do with you, old man?" She wasn't waiting for an answer, wasn't inviting one or inviting him in, just watching from the doorway, disappointed.

Rudy nodded. "You're probably right." He shrunk, shoulders sinking, trying hard with his eyes to show what he was feeling. The Negra saw it, in there, past the broken nose and the heavy lids, was the father of her love, was a piece of Tre, and he hurt.

She hid under cover of her brow, embarrassed, then looked back inside her home. Perhaps just for somewhere else to look or to invite him in. Her arms said she was ashamed of the mess inside, and only then she remembered the knife, still held tight in one hand. "I didn't mean it. It's just—"

She hid the knife behind her back with one hand, trying now to fix her knotted hair with the other.

"It's okay," Rudy said. "We're learning as we go."

Thirty-Eight

The men and women who flocked to the Capitan's house on Sundays were indistinguishable from Nora's imaginings of them, and indistinguishable from each other.

The men had trim mustaches and, though balding, they all had high and tight haircuts that left only ridges of hair high on their foreheads, hardly more substantial than their mustaches and similarly translucent in sunlight. They all spoke in deep voices when they were very pleased and nasal tones when they disapproved of something someone of a higher rank had said, unless that someone of a higher rank were present and had said it to them and then they spoke with no tone at all, Yes, Sir, I hadn't seen it that way until you mentioned it.

The women wore nice bright clothes and spoke brightly of nice things and nothing that meant anything much at all. When Nora brought books into the conversation she ended up stroking her collarbone in the silence for a long while before the young Capitan slid over, his muscles shifting like shadows in his fiercely pressed clothes. She forgot her awkwardness when he wrapped an arm around her, saying, "Her father was a professor."

Then all the rich folks singsonged, "Oh."

Encouraged, the Capitan said, "She wants to be one too."

And then all the rich folks said flatly, "Oh."

They played croquet in the backyard. A walled rectangle of grass with no flowers or trees. But a wooden trelliswork, newly erected and nearly bare, did support the young curls of a grapevine.

"One day we'll drink from those," the Capitan said. He raised a glass to call the crowd's attention. "As husband and wife," he said, smiling. A few said congratulations. They all clapped, but not loudly. When he kissed her the other couples paid too much attention to a bad shot by an older man with a limply handled mallet. Nora kissed the Capitan again, but this time he tugged her away with the hand wrapped clear around her back, so that the effect was to open her up to the couples in the yard, all holding glasses, swishing them around, smirking as if they all knew the couple's fate but wouldn't tell.

The sun: bright. The dress: plain, ugly, yet still somehow uncomfortable. This was a daily requirement: discomfort. He'd told her as much. His duties were to serve, to do without sleep if it meant succeeding in his mission, a mission he'd tell her nothing about, and don't ask. Her duties were to serve in enhancing their public appearance. To be at all times desirable but not coquettish, graceful but not loose, and smart, but deferential to a long list of names she'd never remember and a long list of ranks for which all the badges and buttons looked the same. Hours of the morning so early she considered them night, she burned her thumb on the steam of the iron. Social functions nearly every night where everyone drank, but everyone was so composed that they spoke even less drunk than sober, and without their false humors were crabby at best. Old women dabbed their lipstick on every napkin in sight. She'd imagine the red lip prints as rose petals tossed around whatever dark wood house they were in at the time, and she missed her mother's cloth napkins and the green patio and the colorful garden, and the laundry waving on the line in her mind made her miss her own clothes.

Toward the end of the party, with everyone outside, she escaped into the house. Empty, she thought, until she discovered a young soldier at the Capitan's desk chair. He acknowledged her casually, eyes bright blue with youth and the glass of white wine clutched like a gun at the rim.

"You ought to hold it by the stem," she said.

Already he was sliding shut a drawer in the desk. He smiled and shrugged, raising a comic book with a piece of familiar notepaper as its bookmark. "Bad habits. I'm full of them."

She stood still until he'd left, and then went promptly to the drawer.

Inside, nothing looked out of place.

The notepads were flush atop one another. Past writings only ghostly imprints, a few ink stains.

Pens fit snugly against one another, too, like bullets in a bandoleer.

She slouched into a preposterously high backed chair and let her "carriage," as her Capitan called it, sink, go prickly from the sudden and rare relaxation, and remembered sneaking sits in her father's chair to read the first lines of twenty books in a row.

Was her father still doing nothing but sitting in that chair, not even reading? She gulped a glass of sour white wine and indulged a wince at it and her father both. Him sitting there. In the dark. Letting the once boiling mind go stagnant. She resented him for it, and it wouldn't have happened if he'd thought ahead. Strategized. Played the game with the right defense.

The Capitan was laughing somewhere nearby now, and she stood suddenly and hid the suddenly empty wineglass in a potted plant.

Outside, she saw the Capitan with an old man, both holding mallets, laughing and looking the women over with bright faces and eyes. Her Capitan was forty years younger at least, but the skin beneath his eyes sagged and his cheeks caved and when he laughed, the ridges of his throat looked exposed.

In her home, as for spirit, there'd been decay. And in this man's home, more. The man himself? She thought he was dying each day and she felt in her heart because he was a good man he was dying of guilt, and she feared it wasn't just for her father—though she selfishly hoped that it was—she feared he was dying for having caused far more deaths than she was willing to know. She wondered if, in some way, her father's was one of them.

The Capitan clapped the old man's back and when he turned to face her she'd just returned from getting a bottle for the ladies' glasses as an excuse to pour one of her own, and he didn't find her but looked around, from face to face, quicker and quicker, like there were reason to fear being lost here in his own backyard.

She raised her hand subtly, trying to catch his eye and calm him.

Thirty-Nine

We don't have telephone lines in the barrios of Clearwater. There's only one phone within walking distance and nobody uses it much because we're all within walking distance, and a much shorter walk besides. As for the phone, a once very fat, tall servant man stole it from a fine house before he was fired for stealing much finer things than phones. He charged a nickel, food or liquor for calls, and lived alone in a converted tool shed. Since the day he'd been fired and caterpillared his long thick body up a phone pole near the city hall, spliced his own wire and run it through the sewer, he'd lived off pastries and liquor because no one had many nickels, and he'd withered to nearly a stick. He often walked the neighborhood with a cane and we'd joke which one was the cane. We all called him Calaca.

He wasn't walking when the phone rang. He was slack in a hammock like it was his cocoon, and the little boys playing soccer in the street stopped. They dared one, the smallest one, to answer the phone. Its ring rattled the air and seemed louder each time.

The boy crept into the man's tool shed, huffed his long hair out of his eyes, and lifted the receiver slowly to his ear. He listened with his small lips rounded.

The crackling and electrified voice on the line said, "Hello? Hello?"

In Playas, near the Ocean Club, the faux-tropical band was loud enough that Tre had to plug his ear with one finger, and press the hard phone against the other. A dark vendor sold tacos to a white man in a white suit. Foreign cars painted yellow jammed the street. "Hello?" Tre called into the phone.

In the shed, the boy seemed suddenly aware of just how dark things were around him. The distant and breezy music coming over the phone must have sounded not breezy but ghostly, haunting. The voice ragged, because it was, and desperate, because Tre was that too.

Tre looked around for a street sign. "It's Tre. Get the Negra. It's Tre. I'm not dead. Tell her I'm not dead." Swarms of pedestrian tourists jostled him, snapping pictures of bright smiling locals selling gaudy trinkets that no one but tourists could afford or want to buy. "But I'm stuck. And I'm hurt pretty bad."

The boy, stepping cautiously back from the phone's cradle, had to have known that Tre was gone—disappeared, decesparacedo—and for him, like for most, that meant dead. He had the receiver in his hand but not the cradle, and the cord was going taut, losing spirals with every step. Over the phone, now lowered to the boy's side, Tre's voice was yelling, "Tell them I'm at the Ocean Club."

A board creaked beneath the boy's feet.

Calaca stirred in his cocoon, flung one insect-thin leg out of the hammock, and then another. He shouted at the boy not to move any further.

The boy screamed, ran off so fast with the receiver in hand that the cord yanked out and snapped back. Calaca ducked it like a wasp.

All the boys in the street yelled and followed the smallest boy, still waving the phone high in the air and screaming.

Calaca, free of the hammock, stood out front his tool shed stabbing his cane into the cloudless sky.

When the boys reached the Negra's house the one with the phone looked terrified, but all the rest were smiling and cheering and repeating what the boy had worn his voice raw screaming at them: Tre's spirit is calling, surrounded by ghost music at the bottom of the sea.

Tre had not sung it to them. The other boys had made it a song on the way here.

Don't you hear him? Spirit's calling. From the bottom.

From the bottom.

From the bottom of the sea.

By now, Rudy was driving away from the Negra's, and the boys trailed in the sedan's dust for a while, dogs slipping between their legs, shooting under their feet, until they all fell back one by one and only the little boy remained in miniature in the rear-view mirror, the phone waving.

Rudy's eyes brightened. He even smiled. If Tre were alive he'd be happy knowing that the Negra was safe, was strong, and had refused to leave her neighborhood until Tre came back or she had seen his dead body with her own eyes.

Forty

An ambulance lurched against traffic that wouldn't part for the blinking lights and sirens. Eventually, the driver shut off both and slunk his arm out the open window. There was hardly enough space to pass between cars but Tre hopped a few bumpers and looked casually inside the rear window of the ambulance when he passed, saw that someone was bandaged and tended to by a fat man in a blue uniform.

Tre ducked out of sight, then. Nearly ducked into a tall dirt bike weaving through traffic, the leather-jacketed driver only pausing to pop a wheelie and flip Tre off. When he did, the rider almost lost control. He looked back over a shoulder a few times, but rode on. Something about that rider struck Tre as familiar.

Tre came back to the ambulance and sat its bumper the whole way to the hospital. He only fell off once, they'd only been going about five miles per hour, when a bike taxi crossed in front of them and the ambulance shuddered him loose. Occasionally he waved to drivers or passengers in the cars behind them.

He hopped off before the ambulance circled into the medical center near the university, where a nearby door closed pneumatically on the shrinking figure of a doctor. A cigarette smoked in the ashtray.

Tre slipped into the dim hall that smelled salty and was empty. Only then did he register the dirt bike that had been parked just a few feet outside the door. He backed up and opened the door, took the cigarette up out of the ashtray and smoked it down to the filter, staring at the familiar dirt bike all the while.

He held the smoke in his lungs for a long time after the door had shut him inside once again, and was exhaling it in small puffs when he found a bathroom door.

The water in the shitter was brown. The faucet in the sink, when he turned a knob, did nothing. There was a drain in the center of the tiled floor and scum creeping from it to different destinations on the walls and ceiling. There was a showerhead in one wall, but no curtain or division of any kind, and he felt then the slight slope of the floor to the drain.

He stripped. He locked the door and turned on the shower and, after letting it run brown a minute, the salty water drenched him. He wouldn't open his eyes or let the water touch his dry tongue. He used his elbow on the knob when he turned the shower off. He eventually had to use his hand on the doorknob, though.

There was a man pushing an empty gurney down the hall and Tre whistled to him. The wheels squeaked when the man backed the gurney up and set it against a wall and came down a ways.

"I messed up my…" Tre hoped trailing off would help. Really he didn't know what to call the things he'd seen patients wear on his few visits to hospitals on business, if you could call putting a second hit on stubborn targets business.

"Your gown?"

"Yeah. Shit all down my…" the man was already holding up a hand to stop him and gesturing with the other to say just a minute. He came back a moment later and tossed the gown to Tre.

"I've got to get a patient. I'll be right back to check on you. Okay?"

Tre nodded, mugging his pain. "I'm not going anywhere."

Smiling now, Tre strolled down the hall with a clean body, slick hair, and a gown he was fairly certain was not responsible for the itching he felt in his danker places; he felt like a new man. The only thing he needed was to get his shoulder taken care of. He looked from room to room for a doctor to bullshit but all he found were patients waiting in gowns just like his. The heat down the insides of his thighs, crawling up to his crotch by the minute, spurred him, and his ass quivered in the breezy hall, the straps falling loose either side. When he opened the last door he was gritting his teeth and scratching at his groin.

"Tre?" The voice sounded familiar, but the medical mask made it hard to see anything but the one long eyebrow curling up at the sides in constant surprise. The man removed the mask. It was Junior. He had on a stethoscope, a doctor's paper cap, and scrubs. Underneath the disguise you could tell he was wearing the leather jacket Tre'd bought him.

"Nice outfit."

"Me? What about you?" Junior pointed at the gown, open in back, Tre scratching furiously now.

There was another knock, and Junior put the mask back on. The door opened, and a nurse wheeled a gurney into the room. A man bandaged thickly around the chest and stomach breathed awfully loud through a tube in his nose. A military uniform sat in neat squares piled on his stomach. He looked like he was trying hard to sleep, face tensed and brows sunken. Or to die. He wouldn't have to try hard, because Junior had already tugged the pistol from his waistband. He put two bullets in the patient's head before Tre could blink at the blasts. Junior grabbed Tre's limp arm just as fast and bowled through the screaming nurse clawing her paper cap down over her eyes.

Out into the hall. Tre howled in pain at Junior's grip. The two of them ran recklessly past doctors, nurses, and turned whenever there was a place to turn. The creaking and jangling sounds of security closed in behind them. Only when they had burst through the exit door and hopped on Junior's dirt bike two to the seat, did Tre feel relief run over his skin: Tre's gown blowing in the wind, the breeze cool once they were moving through traffic, the commuters behind them honking and pointing, whistling at Tre's pale flanks.

Forty-One

The Capitan sifted through orders and found the forms he was looking for. Like all of the forms, they were photocopied templates with the information typed in too high or too low on the provided lines. The new recruits that ran the office never got their spacing right, and minor inadequacies like these eased his fears that he would soon be replaced.

He fingered through a pile of forms, thumbed another like a deck of cards. He rolled his chair back and spun around to face a filing cabinet and opened up a drawer. Inside were the blank sheets, the templates, from which he removed two. In a rare hunch over his desk, he copied down the registration number of a plane bound for the ocean to dispose of evidence—items and papers that had the potential to be exhibits in court but, in some higher-up's view, should not. He wrote carefully on the new template the orders that would redirect the plane, and tucked the old copy in his pocket, then waved the newly written one through the air to dry the ink. He took a needed moment to straighten his cramped back.

On his way out of the office he set the papers on a small desk at the end of a long hall. The Capitan's assistant had just dropped into a drawer the broken tape recorder and its ripped work order for repair and gone back to his comic book. There was a sloppily sketched parrot making eyes at an outrageously busty blonde. The blonde's shirt wasn't a shirt so much as her skin colored in blue. The soldier clearly hoped that remaining stationary was the best approach at avoiding any reprimand. He often treated the Capitan like a raptor: if you didn't move, he couldn't see you.

The Capitan said, "Fill in the new one."

"Yes, sir."

The Capitan about-faced and went to the door and when he opened it he snapped his head back in time to see the soldier grinning.

"Private."

"Yes, sir?"

"Do it now. You'll have plenty of time to read comics when you're sitting in that seat all weekend, got me?"

The soldier sighed, folded the comic book in half and tucked it under his leg, "Yes, sir." When the Capitan had gone, he took an electronics catalog from the desk drawer and began browsing through it. He stopped flipping through the pages once, to take up a pen and circle a new tape recorder.

Forty-Two

"Let me off here," Tre spoke over Junior's shoulder.

Junior either couldn't hear him for the wind whipping by or pretended not to.

"Let me off here," Tre shouted.

The bike whined when it downshifted, then the motor sank into a low hum and the barred windows blurring by straightened themselves out, the city arranging itself around them.

"What's going on? You're in bad shape. You don't need to be passing up opportunities like this."

"Opportunities? Man, I ain't seen you in how long and within ten minutes I'm an accomplice."

"I got a new dude. Young military dude got his eye on the prize. Wants to take his boss down. That guy today, corrupt pilot carrying live bodies where they shouldn't be carryin' them. Shit's steady work."

"What happened to standards?"

Junior looked away, shrugged. "Where are you gonna go, huh?"

"Home, I guess."

"Home?" Junior took it as a joke and waved his hand to show he did. "Come on, dog." He took off the leather jacket and pressed it against Tre's chest. "I could buy my own, now."

Tre was as near the metro line downtown as he knew how to get, which could have been pretty far after all. He told himself it was close and kept walking in one direction because this was the type of man he'd grown into. He stuck to decisions out of pride even if the only one around to call him on a change of course was himself, and didn't give more than a moment's thought to what he would have found himself into had he gone with the old friend back to whatever apartment or poor house they lived in to kill and steal and be rich.

There was a yard with laundry hanging like neon signs in the sun, and he hopped the low wall and went to pick something. He found a pair of women's jeans large enough to fit him, a blousy shirt but all of them were blousy, and at least this one was orange. Negra always told him he looked good in orange. He smirked thinking she definitely hadn't meant another woman's shirt. He dropped the leather jacket and stripped off the gown. He held it close and scrutinized the fabric, where a pale furred bug circled a stitch. When he was done examining his pink thighs and groin, he cursed the hospital and swore he'd never go inside one again.

Someone giggled.

When he looked up, the thick figure of a woman cut across the neck by shade was pointing the finer pieces of her body at him. He clutched the clothes to himself and waited for his legs to run him out of there. They didn't. The woman's hand rose into the shade and when it dropped into the sun again it held a cigarette, smoking at the thumb-hooked belt rung of her pants, perched between bright orange nails.

He slid his good arm into the shirt. Let the other arm hang for now, the leather jacket draped over it like a cloak. The pain had faded every hour. He stepped one leg into the jeans, felt himself flop against his thighs as he stepped into the other. He didn't bother with zippers or buttons.

"I've got the right thing for you, darling," she said. He didn't like the way she said darling. She said it the way women said it to other women they knew well but couldn't stand. He remembered the women's clothes he was wearing and flushed a shade of red that clashed with the orange shirt.

She said he looked like a sugary bar drink, and he blushed brighter but the woman was so calm she seemed to calm the air around her. The flies that had buzzed in the alley and the bees near the laundry-line, not a one passed her way.

"I've got to get to the train," he said, a plea.

The hand raised the cigarette and dropped slack and empty. She clacked her orange nails. She giggled again. She stood into the sunlight and walked over. "The train is this way. I'll show you the train. It's a short cut through my yard anyways. Go that way and you might as well walk to the end of the line. Besides, it's bad neighborhood that way." She was already leading him with a hand on his elbow and he was sick from the heat and her thick perfume. She wore too much makeup and though she'd looked thick and young from far away, up close she was starved and made of paper. The makeup on her cheeks looked sprayed on the same way you sprayed walls with stucco.

A short walk past dumpsters. Through a grass yard to a cement slab enclosed on all sides but one by fence. The last side opened onto the back patio of a trailer home. The trailer was in nice condition and the sun beat off it in spots like they were making more sun. Tre squinted, rubbed a dry palm over his damp face, felt a burn setting deep in his skin. "Which way?"

"This way."

"To the train?"

She called a name he didn't hear and the trailer door opened. A slim boy in woman's panties walked pigeon-toed to the fence and hooked his slender fingers through it. His small cock nosed out the side of the panties.

"You like it?" the woman asked.

The boy slid a flat palm down his own chest mechanically, his eyes focused dreamily on a spot somewhere over Tre's shoulder, though at first Tre had thought the eyes were on him and he realized how practiced the boy was.

"Ten," she said.

The boy's hand was slipping down into the panties now.

"Bitch," Tre said.

The woman chastised the boy for a long time loud enough to hear. Tre took the first street sideways and abandoned the direct course for one less depressing. It didn't work. No one knows for sure, but some say it was just coincidence that woman saw him there that afternoon he was looking around for the train. The woman, of course, said it was not, but by then she was completely impoverished and slightly crazy with what most said was syphilis.

He could have slipped onto the top of a train that afternoon, but what helps this version of the story is that it was so hot and those trains could blister an ass if one rode them that way during the day. Plus, sometimes the government used that method of riding as an excuse for arrest and putting you to work. And, sometimes the guerillas used that method of riding as an easy route to forced recruitment. Anyway, it was easy to sunburn and he was already burned and when he ducked into the shade of the street still in earshot of the woman and the boy, he got sick and stayed in the shade a while. Then a while longer. And then it was almost dark and it wouldn't be much longer to wait if he decided to help that boy.

The woman said she had good business that night, and Tre must have heard whatever ugly sounds went along with that business. She claims it was Tre who snuck back around in the dark, found her smoking a cigarette leaned back against the rocking trailer. Her head was rocking too, and Tre helped it along, rocked it hard into the trailer wall.

Then he'd crept into the trailer itself, trying hard to be careful. That had meant watching the big guy do his business to the boy for a moment, the big guy they found later in the empty trailer naked with a slit in his throat from his own knife. The knife was stolen, and Tre, in the man's fitted and fashionable clothes, and the boy, in the now-baggy clothes Tre had been wearing, sat side by side. They sat amongst many refugees on top of a rocking train car, each with an arm looped around the electric pole that ran to the wires across the sky.

Forty-Three

When the Capitan opened the door there were five neat rows of five kneeling bodies, heads covered in grain sacks and wrists tied at their backs. There were others, many others, in many other rooms, but these ones were his. None of them raised their heads. They looked caught in the middle of some act of faithful penance. The room smelled damp, spicy and sour. The walls bore green tattoos of moss from the condensation of sweat, piss, and breath. The floors, though there were rusted drains in them, were slick and darkly moist as well. He stepped into the room, made sure none of his peers were in sight, and shut the door behind.

The Capitan no longer worked the parade deck down at the docks. The troops' purpose had been to contain any possible outburst by the protesters, mostly women, who serpentined through the city with signs, and gathered at the docks to ask the military where their missing loved ones now resided: in a ditch, an ash pit, swaying in gruesome schools at the bottom of the sea? By now a young soldier with nice teeth and shaggy hair that his father, a colonel, let him keep, had infiltrated the protesters. He'd discovered in a church that money had been raised to distribute reports, to presses around the world, of the military government's torture practices. Naturally, the church was raided.

Now the parade deck is only loud when the surf crowds the shore or the wind whips the flag. No soldiers needed there. It's vast and shiny from the wear of the soldiers' boot heels, a blank chessboard. There are no police around—state or otherwise— because there are no people. Even the seagulls gulp their crumbs in the grass at the parade deck's borders, and don't ever circle above it, though the outer edges are frosted in shit. Grey alcoves pock one side of an old grandiose building, and egrets nest inside them like unlit white candles.

Forty-Four

Tre and the boy picked their way through the trashy runs alongside the train, and onto the first major street. They faced an overgrown cemetery from the 40's, when even the dead were segregated—now the only segregations were political, and even that usually an issue of cash or class. The boy stayed always a few feet behind Tre with his head sunk low like a shy or often-beat dog. "Come on." Tre jabbed the boy's shoulder to play, but the boy cowered and Tre told himself not to play that way anymore.

When they got to Tre's parents' house, the soldiers were emptying it of anything valuable. A few sat on the living room chairs in the storage van, a few on the grass smoking skinny cigarettes and laughing. Tre tugged the boy along and walked casually past, fighting hard not to look at any of them and to look miserable enough to ignore. A few neighbors taking the cool air and whittling or gossiping outside their front doors stared at Tre until recognition painted their faces as bright as the moonlight painted the asphalt, tree trunks, and porch railings. Tre raised a finger to his mouth, and kept walking without turning his head.

The boy stared dumbly over a shoulder, limping a little, and one of us said from a porch, "Who's the culero?"

We didn't keep quiet. That wasn't our way. And we were expecting him around back in the alley. Most of us had already gathered around Tre in anticipation, studying him studying his backyard, elbowed up onto the wall in silence. He kept jutting his chin at things in the yard, at the memories moving like ghosts that only he could see. It was like he'd been gone from home for years. Or maybe like he could already see what a few more years would do to his home.

He dropped down from the wall. Clusters of folks whitewashed by the moon stared and whispered, waiting for him to speak. We almost believed Tre had the power to turn a street upside down and shake all its ingredients into a new order, one that lacked any sign of strong-arms or arrests. "Were my parents taken?"

"No. But they will be," an old man said. "The military's claimed the house. Neither your mom nor dad go in or out. It's only a matter of time."

"How long has it been already?"

"Not too long," the old man said. "It's only a matter of time."

"You don't think they've cooperated?"

Some of us thought that they had, but none of us expected their own son to say it. Then Tre shook his head and we all knew he'd regretted it. Regretted a lot. Tre looked down the alley like the near past were a place just a ways back that maybe he could still get to. The boy looked for it too. In this new and free place the boy was at a loss for what to do, how to be, and succeeded in an endearing mimicry of Tre.

Tre shook his head and the boy did too.

"It's too bad," a neighbor with a broomy mustache said. "At least I got to see them take my son."

A fat woman in a bowlegged chair said, "I was luckiest. When they killed my husband I was in the car with him."

"That wasn't the soldiers," someone else said. "That's too sloppy. They'd have arrested him first."

"I'm just saying," she said. Everyone nodded. "That's enough talk about soldiers—"

Then the broomy mustached man said, "At least they didn't get the girl who came looking for you. That was a close one."

Tre asked, "My sister's here?"

"Tu hermana? No, no. She's with the Capitan. This girl was dark as that street when it's wet. She cut the one that grabbed her and she got away. A real beauty."

"Black as a bird's eye," someone said, and the strange image rolled around in Tre's head until he was dizzy from following it and shut his eyes. Had anyone said it at all?

"Are you okay?" a sourceless voice asked. "You don't look too good."

"Basta," another voice said. "Enough talk."

"La Negra?" Tre asked.

"La Negra?" the boy repeated.

And Tre slipped into the first of his fever dreams.

Once, he awoke to a blurred shape of the boy pressing his forehead with a cold wet towel. The water ran into his eyes and his dreams were of snow in Los Angeles and a blue sun. Another time he awoke to the broomy mustached man poking him in the temple with a small figurine he'd whittled into a busty woman that looked like a fertility goddess but he held it up proudly and said it was his wife—she'd been the slightly hefty one sitting in the chair when Tre had arrived with the panties boy. And the man was sorry to've poked him, but "you looked especially dead." After that Tre dreamt of an enormous woman overtaken by greenery and lashed by roots to a cave in the earth and she sent forward creatures that did whatever she couldn't do for herself. She was always pregnant with these creatures, and her belly opened like a heavy-lidded eye to let her see. The eye was black. Tre saw the girlish boy in the black circle dancing with a fat man wearing a robe of blood clasped round his neck. He saw a person on a hospital bed shot in the head by an unseen hand and then he saw the hand and it was his and then he saw the body on the bed and that was his too. Last, he saw the Negra in the black eye, smiling at him after he pinched her bottom and showed her a picture he'd drawn from memory of one of his father's old books, before he awoke gasping in a small square room walled by rough wood through which sunlight blared loudly into his eyes, and he was begging for water and the Negra set aside the book she'd been reading to him, and the boy squeezed a soaked rag over Tre's mouth until he heard the Negra's voice: Go ahead, let him drink. He'll throw up but he'll be okay now.

Forty-Five

It had not even been morning of his third day gone when Tre and the boy returned to the hood, and it was hard to believe so much had changed so quickly. When the children first went looking for Negra, they found instead a sign on her fence that said that the military had come. Some fool had called the police to report the guerillas' attack—the same fool who'd bought the house from the police before Tre and the Negra's beds had cooled, and already the cane had been chopped down to the roots. A chicken coop filled most of the back-yard, the rickety room relocated—shit, rust, and all—so that it appeared to have been there all along. Almost as long as the shed holding Tre's motorcycle, still hiding like some entrenched guerilla's burrow in the tall grass.

It was the Negra who found the children. She'd been keeping watch on the shed because she knew Tre would have wanted her to, and because she'd hoped that he would come back. She panthered up behind them, snuck a forearm under one's chin, cradling his head and brandishing the knife at the others. The smell of pickled eggs filled the air and the Negra looked down the boy's front to see his dark crotch and the puddle growing round his right foot. She cringed for his pride, but only once the children had told her why they'd come did she lower the knife. "Take me to him. Now."

When she stepped into the dim room a heat splashed Tre's face and soaked him so that he felt he was wet, but he knew his skin was cool when she touched his cheek. He wasn't feverish anymore, just happy to have her.

He slept uneasily that night, woke when it was still dark, and snuck out to walk to his parents' house to find some of the windows boarded up. There was a light on in the kitchen window, and boards lay beneath it in the flowerbed. There was a sign on the door that said the house was government property and that any subversive action on government property was not only a crime but also one punishable by death. It stated that any and all houses in the area fell under the same stipulations. He knew that meant the one he lived in now, too.

This was one of the ways the government kept their territory small enough to manage, strangling communities not to death, exactly, if they learned to live on less air. The government bought up houses between the corporate sector downtown and the resorts on the coast, and they set the buildings for demolition that never came directly, though infrastructure crumbled. Instead of mushroom-clouding towns, they exploded the foundation. The dazed souls looked always wandering, vacant-eyed, whether wiping a CEO's car window, or serving a Colonel's mistress a Tequila Sunrise.

He would not end up like them.

When he returned, slamming the door behind him, Negra asked, "Like who?"

"Nobody," he said, and tossed her the first book he could reach on a shelf.

She spent days reading to him until he was able to focus his eyes long enough to read for himself. She walked the long dirt road out of this neighborhood, into hers, past her old house now noisy with chickens and constantly glowing with a halo of white feathers, past the man's shack where the phone had been kept, following the path all the way to the library.

An old man regarded her from the top of a stepladder, asked her name and where she lived and who the books were for, and told her she could take anything she wanted. She asked if he was going to write any of it down. He tapped his temple. "I just did."

Then it was that same path in reverse in the dark, and Tre, who'd reversed his schedule during his fever, would wake from his sleep through the hot day, and read in the cool night air beside an oil lamp, the Negra braiding her hair beside him and asking him to tell her the stories in his own way.

The boy, who now spent most days playing with the kids in the neighborhood, did the daily errands and one of those was to read to Tre and the Negra when he first woke in the morning. Before long, with the sun beginning to weigh so heavy it seemed to stamp the early morning dust into the hard-packed dirt, Tre would fall asleep for the day. They were still afraid to go near Tre's old house.

This went on for days until finally Tre joked that his mind had sucked all the nourishment it could take and now his body needed some too. He made love to the Negra instead of sleeping that day, and the boy and the other neighborhood children giggled outside the house. The man with the broomy mustache, who was letting them live in a room of his, blushed and moved from his seat to the grass a few feet away.

They made it a habit to read in the day then, and the boy brought more kids with him everyday, and everyday there were more chairs in the front yard. The Negra improvised a new way to string the laundry in the front yard so that most of the day the yard was walled in by cool white sheets and the roof was the foliage of a tree rooting out into the useless road more each day.

Once, when the Negra arrived at the library, the old man climbed down his stepladder and shuffled over to the Negra, standing by a window, and looked outside before drawing the curtains. "They came."

"Who came?"

He shrugged. "Who knows? Guerillas. Military. Politicos. One dressed as another. They asked to see the records. They asked who checked out the books."

Negra grabbed the old man's wrist. "What did you tell them?"

"The truth." The old man tapped his temple. "That I don't keep records."

"And?"

"And a lie. That no one in these barrios knows how to read."

She let go his wrist and he rubbed it, saying, "Ah, that's some grip."

"It's my husband I could lose."

"All these times I've seen you, I didn't know you were married."

"That's alright," the Negra said, taking up a stack of books. "He doesn't know either."

Soon all the children in the neighborhood, twenty or so, ranging from small to tall and young to nearly adults by the standards of the parents—and some parents did complain that the house and yard were failing and what good was reading when there was work to be done by the children—would sit on chairs they'd brought or in the grass. From his place on the porch, Tre watched them at their exercises—exercises his father had pushed upon him, and which he'd skipped out on most of the time. He observed that the ones in the grass looked sullen and performed poorly. They hardly raised their hands, and he thought it was because they couldn't stand to have all the seated students looking down on them at once. After a few days, if no chair or desk-like furniture could be improvised for their small breezy schoolyard, the numbers sitting in the grass would dwindle. He'd be leading a discussion on Pedro Paramo and the role of revolution, when the yielding sheet walls would flutter in, swell out, breathing, inhaling the sound of those past students out playing in the streets. The students seated in neat rows now—Tre hadn't had to tell them to do that, they'd done that themselves—went glazy-eyed and the Negra would have to promise them each a pastry if they paid better attention. She was the disciplinarian most times, and Tre liked that he didn't have to be. But he often twisted grass off its roots and sat there on the porch wondering how even she seemed to weaken when it came to disciplining the children. She never weakened with him, though. She smacked him on the head as she went inside, told him just because he was losing his hair was no reason to do the same to the grass. The children swallowed their laughs and paid too much attention to their books, the way Tre remembered doing if ever his parents bickered, though they rarely had. Tre wondered where his father and mother would end up, and if somehow here he and the Negra were replacing them. It felt proper and crude, natural and somehow deviant, not to watch a shadow stretch away until it was no longer there but to simply stand at the right angle so your shadow superimposed itself and the other was gone forever. Or maybe the shadow wasn't gone. Maybe shadow upon shadow could become so thick they formed a person and that's how all people were formed.

He had lost more than six students to the evolution of values in the town that said to sit in the grass at school—the students called the house that now—was worse than being the poorest or darkest kid in the neighborhood. It hadn't helped matters at all that the darkest kid was named Chato and he brought his grandfather's rocking chair each day and was one of the best students.

One morning Tre woke up before the Negra. He pulled on a loose tee-shirt and sweatpants—he'd given up shoes for a while now, since he didn't move about the city so much.

"You want me to make coffee?" she asked from bed, rubbing the sleep from her eyes. "What time is it?"

"Get some rest. Have the kids play through the morning."

"Where are you going?"

"To see my parents."

"Why now?"

"We need new books. We've almost been through the library's and besides, I heard they're watching it now. It's too dangerous for you."

"You want to see home. Don't use me in your lies."

He smirked at how well she knew him. "Don't you think it's been too long already?"

She didn't say if she did or she didn't, she just told him to make sure he didn't do something stupid like get caught, and to bring back some eggs from the chicken coop out back of her old house.

"That fat man doesn't give them up for nothing," Tre said, leaning down to kiss her cheek.

"Then take them."

"I don't steal."

She laughed. She looked at his bare hairy toes and laughed harder. Tucked her head under the pillow.

"I'm serious now," he said, hiding one foot under the other. "I don't steal anymore."

"It's just eggs and he's a man that ain't easy to like. I'm happy I helped change you, but don't change too much, yeah?"

"Yeah," he said, and slunk out the door into the white light of morning.

"Put some shoes on your feet," she shouted after him. The shoes struck his back not long after the words had, and he turned, smiling, to see the Negra standing there, the sun through the trees raining gold coins on her naked body.

He told her that he loved her. "But you know that already."

She nodded.

He went to the chicken coop first, because the Negra's old house was farther away but really because he was putting off seeing his parents. The chicken coop occupied most of the yard now—it spanned about ten feet in either direction and was the height of a tall man—and it looked built on a foundation of white marble until you saw that it was just shit. Inside, hens gargled and squawked. It was only about fifteen feet from the house to the coop, but you could approach from behind and be blocked from view. The fat man was adamant that the government had sold him the entire lot and that meant that anything that was on it was his. This wasn't his only lot. He'd made a killing buying up lots that the government seized to thin ranks but didn't need or want. The front yard was busy with people coming and going, and they were all the same types of people, just in subtly different types of clothes that meant they were doing either business or pleasure. They weren't bad people, just indifferent, and snobbish in ways only those too near poverty can be. They lingered around smoking cigarettes with their noses in the air but rather than seem important it seemed they were trying to keep their heads above water. The house had been redone, a big window put in the kitchen to face the back yard, and Tre could see folks moving around the table in there, and new stucco mottled with chicken feathers every few inches. It wasn't until he'd sat on his heels in what little sugarcane was left out back, to watch for the fat man, that he heard the boy creeping up behind him.

"I thought you must be sick," Tre said.

"Me?" The boy crouched beside him.

"Yeah. You didn't bother me all morning."

They pushed each other once each and then Tre raised a finger to his lips. He pointed at the old tool shed. "You know what's in there?"

"What?"

"A motorbike."

The boy scoffed and rolled his eyes the way he must have once seen his haggy pimp do. "Sure."

"Really. You get us a dozen eggs and I'll get us a motorbike, and if neither of us get caught, we'll have a damn good day."

The boy was nearly standing now, forgetting himself with excitement, and just as he stood Tre tugged him down again. "Don't float off like a balloon. Use your head, yeah? We got a deal."

"I gots to get twenty eggs out the coop and that's all?" The boy no longer wore the woman's clothes; Tre'd gotten him as new clothes as he could find. But they fit him too tight and his gestures were always too florid, too cultivated, and the boy strained to be natural in a way that gave him an unnatural grace.

"Who told you twenty was a dozen?" Tre asked.

The boy blushed. He shot a glance over a shoulder as if to say, back then, before you.

Tre looked away. "You only need twelve."

"That's it?" The boy shook Tre's hand and said deal. He brushed his hair back of his ear with a pinky. Tre shook his head at that and crept through the cane to the shed.

A bald patch of dirt ran between Tre and the shed, and he didn't like moving in plain sight the whole time. Still, he figured if they were busy at breakfast he could get the bike easy enough, until he got to it. The shed was locked.

He ducked around until he found a large enough rock, and took it to the door gripped in one hand, looking over his shoulder. The chickens squawked restlessly—he had to be quick. He banged the lock once, twice, then a few more times rapidly until the loop split from the body and he yanked the whole thing out. When he tossed the rock over his shoulder he couldn't help but think he'd brained the boy by accident, because a scream interrupted the red vision of his motorbike almost leaning itself into motion. Tre had been so long without it, he bit his lip, but turned and saw a flurry of feathers around the coop like a tattered fog. Then he heard the fat man yelling.

"Chicken fucker!"

Tre rolled the motorbike out of the shed and hopped on. He kick-started the engine and it coughed but held. Somewhere something needed adjusting, and he was sad he didn't instantly know what and where it was like he would have months ago.

The boy screamed and the coop rattled and the hens' flapped. The fat man's voice was raw from yelling, "I'm gonna fuck you up the ass and see how you like it."

The boy was screaming, "The egg sac, the egg sac. It don't hurt them in the egg sac."

There was a sound like meat plopped onto a cutting board. Then a crash. The gate swung open and the boy rushed out like a giant chicken himself, pale and thin legged trying to hike up his pants with one hand and hold a few eggs in the yellowed and slippery palm of the other. Shit caked one side of his face and so many feathers stuck to him he looked like he was trying not to run but to fly.

"Quit squawking and get on," Tre said.

The boy hopped on the back of the motorbike and hugged Tre with a cheek pressed to his back. "I only got six."

"I guess you were busy."

The fat man chased them as far as the old cane but then they lost him on the overgrown dirt rut Tre had put in the cane so long ago.

"Can I drive?" the boy asked.

"The deal was a dozen, not six eggs and six pregnant hens."

The boy said, "My face left an imprint on the back of your shirt."

"Oh."

"It looks a little like the Virgin Mary."

"What is it? Sweat?"

"When the man caught me he knocked me down on my face."

"It's shit?"

"Yeah. Looks a lot like Mary, though."

"A miracle."

An egg rolled down Tre's stomach to his leg and cracked on the asphalt in their trail.

The boy looked back. "We lost another one. My hand is slippery."

"Got a good enough grip on those chickens."

Tre's grip on the doorknob was tighter than it needed to be, and hard to release once he'd let himself inside—letting go would mean he'd finally let himself come home.

He was alone in the dark, as he had been many times when still a boy. But now, that his parents had not woken up yet felt like—instead of fright—warm milk in his belly. He could tell by the feeling of open space that the soldiers had looted all but the books, and the floor was so barren it didn't feel like his parents' home. It felt like a museum with so little to touch and to see that their history itself seemed made up, pieced together for a hoax.

Tre had left the boy down the street, hiding from the soldiers that had been in the area more and more often, patrolling or taking over houses like this one. With loose lips, Tre made the sound of his motorbike's engine, and stepped tentatively to the main bookshelf in the living room. He was trying to build up the courage to go down the hall and wake his parents, of whom he'd become more suspicious. Lately, with soldiers around, he found it more and more strange that his parents hadn't been taken, their house ransacked or overrun. The house had been looted, sure, but there were houses around town that had been used for a few weeks as barracks and when the soldiers left there was hardly a frame for the family to return to. He remembered one, just a single wall with a window and its curtains in the wind.

He would pick out the books he'd come for first. This would give him something to talk about with his parents. Something besides the obvious to tell them about his life. He would then have to tell them what they already knew. These forgone sins were the hardest to confess, the ones out in the open all along, because your shame had been given time to take root, and you were bound to loose some of your heart's soil when you uprooted it.

Tre slipped his fingertips down the spines of a few books, tilted his head to read some titles. Once when he was a boy he'd arranged all the books by the color of the spine and it had made the room look very pretty. His mother thought it a lovely idea, but she'd always thought of the bookshelves as just one more thing to dust. That night his father and sister demanded that he put the books back in alphabetical order, flustered and hissing mad that they could not find the books they'd needed right away. Tre—a little boy—pointed. "But it's right there. In blue." Rudy and Nora shook their heads and stomped out of the living room. They scoffed to each other: "Blue?"

Tre said it now: blue. He missed his family, taking book after book from the top shelf, setting memory after memory carefully at his feet. The corner of one book heavy on the toe of his shoe. On the shelf—a few books gone, a few toppled—one book seesawed over an object that didn't catch the light so much as create more shadow, an eye blind to his repentant face, his aching brow, the murmuring pain in his trigger finger as he raised it to that object beneath that toppled book, within his toppled home. He touched the chamber of his .38 pistol. Its blind eye was not an eye at all, just an empty hole, and he knew that the eye that had been most blind to his repentance was his own. He did, he did see a way to make up for it all, if he could convince them not as a son but as in some ways what he still was, an enemy. "Get out of here," he shouted. "While you still can. We're coming. Me and my soldiers are coming for the last of you. So get out. Leave while you can. You'll never be rid of us."

A blast might as well have shot off in his face; from the pistol, the shame, the guilt. He made the books fly across the room, their bindings flapping more furious the harder Tre flung them. Tre turned abruptly, and studied the many abused books scattered across the floor, no longer barren but bombed into a kind of chaotic life. He couldn't help but rush to right things. Back on the shelves, back on the shelves with smooth pages, all of them.

"Hello?" his father called feebly from down the hall. "Who's there?"

"Hello?" he heard his mother whisper.

Tre hadn't heard their voices in so long, and hadn't expected it to be like this when he finally did. Their voices tugged him, and he took a step back to steady himself, his vision scanning down the bindings of book after book, title after title, word after word until his head swarmed with letters. He could run to them now, like a child would. He could hope that, if he pretended, they could pretend too, to see him as a boy and innocent. But words began to form in his vision again. Titles arranged alphabetically. He could never make sense of how he'd arranged his life. He could never forgive it. How could he expect anyone else to? Tre held the .38 in his hand, so much heavier than he remembered. Still, what he would do to remain hidden was almost second nature. Like the spit in his mouth, the words came to him.

"Silencio," he shouted into a cupped palm, a palm he'd already found at his face, catching the tears there. "Silence. Back to sleep or it's forever. This is our property now, remember?"

There was a moment of hesitation, but then, "Yes, sir," his father and mother said softly, and Tre listened to them shut the door.

Tre was quiet coming out of the house, and it was only because he was so quiet that he heard the hissing sound of tobacco burning. Across the street, in the grey morning, a uniformed man stood smoking a cigarette. In the glow of that cigarette, you could see that the man was young. He nodded to Tre, lifted a device in his hand to his mouth, and strolled off talking to himself. Tre took this as his cue to move on. After all, many of the soldiers had taken to living in the abandoned offices surrounding the square. Who knew what diseases the square's birds caused, and what damage the diseases did, among other things, to the body, to the mind.

Once Tre and the boy had parked the bike in the raised dust and float-ing feathers, all the children gathered around the boy to hear the story that had produced such a wild end. Tre took the eggs from the boy, who was gesturing too frantically to be trusted with them, and waded through the children to the Negra waiting in the door. They kissed. They watched the boy tell the story like some crazed animal shaman, feathers flitting in his hair and from his arms.

The Negra said, "Only five?"

"No room for more."

"Room for a bike?"

"I'm gonna sell it. We could use the money." He slapped the dark pistol into her caramel palm. "This too. I'll never use it."

The Negra laughed and took the .38 inside, her bare feet slap-ping off toward the kitchen. "I'll put it away with that tacky leather jacket," she called over one shoulder.

Tre watched the children a little while longer, in awe of their faces in awe of the story the mad chicken priest was weaving, and he felt responsible for more than he could say at that moment. He resigned himself to a simple hope. Tre hoped that the boy left out the part about the egg sacs, even if it didn't really hurt the chickens.

Forty-Six

Tre's students sat cross-legged on the floor of the house they borrowed from the old man, and now there were so many that they overflowed back into the kitchen, and down the long hall into the bedrooms, where Tre began dividing them into age groups. One room was for the youngest, and the Negra played learning games with them. They stacked stones with the letters of the alphabet painted on them. She read them duct taped children's books thrown out by the small library near the city hall.

The ones that were young but could now read and write, Tre instructed in the living room, and at the end of each week he collected the books into tall piles and redistributed them in a different order.

"Mr. Sellers?" A skinny kid raised a hand. "Can I have the Márquez again?"

Tre's boy said, "He already read the Márquez."

The skinny kid balked and strutted around the living room flapping his elbows. "Well, you'll be too busy with the chickens."

Tre intervened. "The Márquez. The Márquez. There are others besides that goddam Márquez, you know." We could all guess as to why mentioning Márquez always got a rise out of Tre, having to hear his father and sister go on as they always had. But there was something else to it, too. "He's too fucking wordy. 'Many years later' is the farthest I've ever gotten, and who starts a story that way? That's an ending."

There still had to be something else he hated, that he refused to tell the children, about Márquez.

The Negra always said it was the magic that killed him.

Tre told them there weren't enough books anyway, and after a few weeks or months they'd be reading the same over again, and not to rush to that point because it would be sad then, not happy. The boys all quieted down. They filed out of the house into the empty yellow day waiting, calling them to kick up its dust. Most of them lingered around the house instead, found shade, and folded themselves up beside each other with books. Tre felt bad about ending the day on a sour note. His father had been prone to the same kind of rational thinking that served as a poor substitute for imagination and often as an excuse for pessimism. Tre told himself he'd keep his mouth shut about any days to come if he couldn't see those days as something worth seeing. It would take quiet, though. A quiet inside that he wasn't sure he knew.

He heard the children when he got in bed with the Negra at night, already sleeping and still curling up to him by reflex. The children learned things not from him but from books, and there was nowhere to take that learning and put it to use. They tossed stories back and forth like a game on the porch. Sometimes Negra gasped at her own nightmares, nightmares she would later pretend she'd never had. Tre knew the nightmares were about his sanity and his safety, that she hoped he would go no further in his rebellion and that he hadn't gone too far already. He couldn't help feeling a pang of that old destructive spirit in his chest, like inside there was a version of himself thrashing and clawing, raking the bars of his ribs with a shank.

Another day, Tre and the children sat idly around the old man's house. Thankfully, no one held a book in plain sight—Tre drawing, children playing cat's cradle with old shoe-laces, the Negra braiding her hair.

The wind didn't touch them, the same way it refused to rustle the leaves above, but it was the rustle of pages they missed most.

A young soldier came by smoking a cigarette, clutching a comic book and watching them. He was the same soldier Tre had spotted outside his parents' home. Young but not soft, the smoothness of his face made him hard, like glass. The children whispered insults at him. Their favorite thing to call him was, of course, Chicken Fucker.

When he looked up, they stopped to watch him speak into the device in his hand.

"Do you think he heard us?" Tre's boy asked. "I think he heard us."

Tre walked over to speak with him. They stood by the tree, where its roots reached into the cracked dirt road. "I recognize you," Tre whispered. "That night. Outside my parents' house."

The young soldier rolled the comic book up, and tapped Tre on the chest. "I don't care if your sister marries the President, understand?"

So it was true what Tre had heard, about Nora and the Capitan. The rumors were that they were to be married in the coming weeks, and that the Capitan was the same man who had arrested their father.

"I hope more than you that it's just rumors, you know?"

"You have no idea…" He smoked the cigarette then flicked it down and ground it out with his boot heel. "…the things I hope for."

The soldier walked away and Tre looked back at the kids who were walking back to their own houses. He called out to them, reminding them not to go through the square. He was the only one anymore who remembered about the diseased pigeons.

The children ignored him, going home whichever ways were quickest. Even if that meant wading through the birds in the square, some of which, like piles of stones, weren't seen moving anymore. They were parts of the place for as long as the square would be a place.

The only person who did listen to Tre, who must have overheard (how often must they have spied on him?), the only figure skirting the bird-filled square, was the young soldier. He stopped once, and just to toss something into the gutter. The colorful pages of the comic book fluttered there.

The next day soldiers came clutching tattered papers they called warrants and dragged Tre from bed. The Negra, though, had been ready. She'd sensed not only her man's uneasiness but she sensed an uneasiness of place. The weather had been too hot in the mornings and nights, too cool in the afternoons. It was as if the neighborhood itself, our streets and creaking houses and shacks and wilting trees and drying grass, were telling us the way it would go. So when the soldiers came, as the guerillas had before, in the night, the Negra shot them dead, all three.

Tre was naked in the corner of the small room, bleeding beneath the eye but otherwise fine. He pulled his heel back so the blood seeping across the floor would not touch it. The Negra was standing on the bed trying to catch her breath and to keep her elbows locked, holding the .38 far from her shaking body.

Outside, the military jeep was still running. The boy stood behind it, the exhaust burning his calf red, and he was looking out for anymore soldiers.

Forty-Seven

Maybe it went like this:

This time the Capitan's hammock in his patio was empty and Nora treaded across the grass to the grape arbor, where tight green curls of vine bobbed in the windy moonlight. He sat at the head of the table beneath the arbor, his hands palms down on the table, a host to no one.

"What is it?" she asked.

"Shhh." A finger to his lips. He was watching the cart in the dark past the arbor. A large cage filled it and, inside, the doves slept. Their cooing subdued, whispering. "They sound nice, don't they?"

She sat on the bench-seat at the table, and placed a hand over one of his. "I don't want to release them."

"What do you mean? Why not?" His posture crumbled, his face nearing hers, and she felt that this sudden change in plans was maybe more than he could take, with all the plans he'd been making in the air, so to speak.

"When the bird keeper brought them, I asked if they'd return here, and she said no, they'd be free." She studied the dim white shapes in the cage, smoky, dispersible. "They're not used to it out there. They'll die."

"We aren't talking about the birds, are we? They'll be fine. And as for the birds, I promise, they'll come back here. That's why they're here in the first place."

"She said they wouldn't."

"She was treating the bride to a little romance. They'll be free? She'd go out of business. Ha. No. I promise. I'll prove it to you. But only if you marry me."

"They'll be all right?"

"I'm not the only one in bad shape tonight, am I?"

She stood now. "They leave tomorrow."

He smiled at her as if she were already standing in the arched doorway of the church. Even so, the smile contained a crimp of apology for the life he had brought her, and the family life he had taken. "I'm sorry they can't come to the wedding. But it's for the best. That would be asking for the wrong kind of attention."

"Would you go and make sure everything's okay?"

"To the house?" He ran a hand through his messy hair.

"Would you pick them up yourself?" She came to him and smoothed out the collar of his sleeping shirt.

"Oh, that wouldn't be asking for the wrong kind of attention at all, would it?"

"But, Love?"

"And if I'm late to our own wedding?" He smiled weakly, and blinked once. His hair had grown longer and more limp, hadn't it? She watched it rise for a moment in the breeze teasing the curtains on their distant bedroom window.

"I can't exactly get married without you." She smiled, but it faded quickly. His eyes had gone dull. His focus on the birds deepened. She gathered her thin nightgown around her and whispered, "Now you tell me what's wrong."

He gripped the hand she'd only just set on his cheek. "And what could be wrong, with you here?"

"Thank you, my love," she said, and stroked his face. "My baby."

Forty-Eight

Tre and the Negra packed quickly, taking little with them but some clothes, and Tre the books he was in the middle of reading. Lately a sense of urgency filled him, and one book wasn't enough. He told the families to leave or else they'd all be killed. He told us the military would clean the place out. We didn't listen.

"Why don't you tell your family that?" some of us said.

"It's too late," Tre said, loading duffel bags made of tied off shirts and pants into the back of the jeep. "Or they already know it. Probably both." But we all knew he didn't believe it.

Tre begged us to go. The children gathered round, tugging at his arms, and begged him not to. After a while some of the adults called their children inside to their chores and we all said that it was for the best that he had gone, he was teaching our children to be lazy anyway, and finally some things would get done.

Laundry hung on the lines. Stew bubbled in pots. Crisp brooms swept dirt floors smooth and oiled shears pruned trees off fences. The wilted leaves blowing through the morning made nice shapes: dervishes and folklorico dance patterns in the roads we hardly noticed. With Tre gone, we weren't keeping watch anymore.

Forty-Nine

Tre parked the stolen jeep beneath a familiar overpass, somewhere in a riverbed in the Jungle. The hung body above them could have been tattered laundry, except for the thin white ribs like quills, and the jawbone on the cement below.

Tre, the Negra, and the boy, sloped down into the valley, Tre holding the books and the Negra holding the boy's hand. In the corridor of cool green buildings, voices passed through windows and steps scurried inside the many-windowed apartments. A breeze whispered. Dogs sauntered with easy rhythm across a path into a narrow alley, clean and quiet, where a woman beat the dust from a blanket using a split baseball bat.

Boys waited at the corner where Tre had taken that ride to Playas, and he asked them where he might find whoever was in charge here. They all craned their necks to look at the Negra and the boy. Tre snapped his fingers for their attention, and one boy tongued a missing front tooth and said, "In charge?"

Tre said, "You know. A mayor. Or Captain. Someone with guns."

The group of boys blinked at him. A truck arrived and the boys scrambled on its bed. They all pointed to the same place.

An American flag flew from the top of a rickety pole in the yard of
the house at the end of the main drag. Its stripes were strips of sepa-
rate cloth, sewed together, and its stars were made of tin—when the
flag curled in the wind they rattled. The flag flew above a simple
house apart from the complexes that lined the road. It wasn't painted,
but a fine dust softened its appearance. It took the sun like it needed
it, was a bright place in this town of mostly shade.

Tre knocked on the open door.

There were a group of men talking around a table, discolored
notebooks open before each of them, pens in their hands. The conversation ceased, and Tre felt an intense heat on the back of his neck.

"Who are you?" The man speaking was old but powerful, gripping the arms of his chair at the head of the table. A pot of stew sat
in the table's center, and before each man at the table was a bowl and
a hunk of bread. Tre's belly roiled loud enough in the silence that the
old man smirked. "Hungry, huh?"

"My name is Rudy Sellers. They call me Tre where I'm from,
which ain't too far. I was hoping me and my family could stay here."

"You ex-military?"

"No, sir."

"You're a guerilla?"

"No, sir."

"What are you running from?"

"Both of those things."

Every man at the table chuckled. Tre's lip twitched.

"Good. Good. Well, what do you do?"

Tre thought for a while. What did he do? It used to be he could
answer that question fast as a bullet, usually with one. But now? He
brushed his thumb over the book in his hand. An old leather-bound
one with the title worn off the outside.

"So you're a charity case. Good. We didn't think we had enough
of those."

"I'm a teacher."

All the men in the room laughed.

Rudy looked back at the Negra and she bugged out her eyes in a way that said look at them, not me. He snapped his head, stood up straight, and said, "I'm a teacher."

"A teacher? Not politics, I hope."

"Reading," Tre said. "Writing."

The man stood, an old baggy pea coat swinging its hem at his thighs. Under the coat, where Tre expected a collar and pins, all he found was a tee-shirt, its collar stretched. "There's a woman at the end of this block who takes boarders. You can stay with her until you get settled in." Tre began to turn when the man said, "Why'd you come here and ask me?"

"I was looking for whoever was in charge."

"It's a town. You could have just asked for a place to stay from anybody."

The Negra took the boy back into the front yard behind him. Tre shifted. "I don't know any places like that."

"Now you know this one."

Tre smiled at that.

"Are any more of your people coming?" the man asked him.

My people, Tre thought. But didn't know how to answer.

"Reading?" the man asked, squinting over the books in Tre's hands. "You've got your work cut out for you."

Tre thought about his other options, the old ones.

"It's not work," Tre said. "Trust me." But he wasn't there anymore. He was thinking like his old self for a moment. He was back in that hospital room with Junior, studying the crisp folds of that military uniform in a neat stack on the bed. That was the only thing neat about it. A dirty hit for some military man, Junior had said, who was trying to make a rise. Grounding pilots for carrying live cargo.

"My eyes are gone," the man said. "You mind hanging around a few until the sun sets? We're old and we fuck up and get the flag on the grass. Last week Martin here got dizzy from looking up too long. You get it down and send the family off and we'll talk a little while."

Tre knew dizziness. Lost in his hood's square crowded end to end with his people. His family was there. His sister, in his mind still a little girl pale from too much time reading inside, stared at him blankly from behind a veil, until the Capitan lifted it. His father reading to his mother, her not listening even a little, humming an old tune instead: kiri kiri ki, Paloma, kiri kiri ki, no lloras. Kiri kiri ki, little dove. Kiri kiri ki, don't cry. Laughter. Junior, that big dog, grinning and whispering into a detached bloody ear, "Come here, I've got a secret."

"Send the family off," Tre heard the man in the pea coat say now. But all of it was past, present and future in his head. His parents would be leaving, he knew. Leaving. But something was wrong. How were they going to get out, to leave the country? And who had been watching Tre leave that night he'd gone into his parents' house for the books? The crazy young soldier who talked to himself.

Now Tre was the one talking to himself, trying to figure it all out. Tre sent the Negra and the boy off to get a place to sleep. He sat on a rock in the yard and watched the flag hanging limply on the pole. Inside, the men passed around a bottle of something, and spoke about things in hushed and serious tones. The sun dimmed even on this house in the open, and the sky reddened in the west. A breeze sailed the flag that way, the stripes rich, and Tre stood and went dutifully to the short pole not much taller than a tall man, began to unwrap the rope from its hook, soldered together out of rusty clothes hangers.

Fifty

In the grey morning the soldiers marched through Clearwater square, some of them firing shots at the birds, feathers bursting.

Others smiled and scattered poisoned seed by the handful.

All around them the birds flapped and swooped just above the fractured cobblestones.

The soldiers remarked that it was a pleasant town, when they moved into its streets. They all took bouncing steps. Gazing around as they were, like you'd do in a garden, their skirmish formation called to mind a group of lifetime friends, out on a stroll, carrying rifles instead of walking sticks.

Fifty-One

Tre shook the Negra awake.

She panicked for a moment, looked around the strange simple room.

He looked out the window at the blue morning. No birds sang. No planes flew in the sky, yet. "Shhh," Tre said. "It's early." He felt bigger in that leather jacket, heavier. When he hugged her, she sniffed the jacket and made a face but he ignored her. "Where's the gun?"

"In the glovebox of the jeep." She poked the heavy leather jacket, felt the armored plates inside. "What are you doing in that thing?"

"Why do you do that?"

"Do what?"

"Ask questions you already know the answers to."

"Because a man's only happy when he thinks he knows more than his woman," she said, and flipped him off and blew him a kiss at the same time.

"I'm afraid someone's figured out their plan to escape. I'm going to bring them back here instead. It'll be quick. I promise."

Her brow was black with a tangle of wrinkles. "I'm coming."

"You should know better."

"Why not?" She sat up in the bed.

He pointed to the boy curled up on the floor. "It's the first day of school, no?" And he reached out to pinch her.

She smacked his hand away. "Apurate," she told him. Hurry. Get out of here. She meant hurry back.

What he did was he blew her a kiss from the doorway. "I'm already gone."

Fifty-Two

It gets harder and harder to be sure, but we're sure of this: the Capitan arrived at the house with little fanfare. The dust didn't rise in the dawn-damp road. Soldiers walked the streets, some laughing, but most of them enjoyed the quiet, burst only here and there by dwindling rifle shots taken at the last remaining birds in the square.

The Capitan checked the rear-view mirror once, twice, watched the street ahead for a while. Two soldiers smoking cigarettes walked in his direction. He was a Captain, he reminded himself. He must have needed reminding, as fragile as he looked, as dark as his eyes were when he checked the empty street in that rear-view mirror one more time. When he left the jeep running the exhaust was white, and dripped thick drops into the street.

In the bedroom, Leticia was helping Rudy dress because despite Leticia's self-imposed solitary, and despite her missing and presumed dead boy, and despite what could have been called a betrayal by her daughter, these things, or thinking of them, did not deflate the near-to-bursting feeling in her chest. The feeling of escape.

Sitting in front of her vanity mirror, she ran a large comb through her black hair. She took great care with it, holding a thick band tight and working the hair until it shone like obsidian. Over her shoulder she could see Rudy sitting as she'd left him on the bed, with one arm through a sweater, the other arm of the sweater left dangling. His brow was far more wrinkled than it had been when he'd entered the jail. Leticia tried reminding him more than once that there was nothing good left here.

Rudy grinned a stiff toothy grin, rose, and went to touch Leticia's face reflected in the mirror. "One might say I don't share your sentiment. There are loose ends."

"You and your loose ends," Leticia said quickly. "I'd feel it."

"I've heard talk around town."

"He would have come," she said flatly, and began to punish her hair.

"You of all people should believe," Rudy said, turning from the mirror now, showing her his hunched back.

He was stuck there, the loose arm of the sweater at his side.

"Finish putting on that teacher's sweater. I know things too," she said, and attacked a new band of hair. "For instance, I know things in real life don't happen like in your books." Her mirrored image showed the back yard to her through the window, the shady avocado tree she used to lay under with her kids—Leticia sensed that Rudy was avoiding laying eyes on all of it—and before too long she began to brush her hair with her eyes closed.

Tre parked the jeep a few blocks from the house, where most of the cane beside the dirt roads ended, and the streets had already begun to thicken with soldiers. His chances were better hopping fences. It hadn't been that long. He steered clear of the square entirely, taking the first alley and from there, a short climb over a chain link fence.

When he landed, the forgotten .38 flew free of the leather jacket's pocket, struck the ground, and blasted the air open.

He dove to the ground and clutched the thing like you might a crying baby. Soldiers' voices rose in volume, in frequency, and when he sprang on through the tall grass of a yard toward yet another fence, he felt like he was nearing a hive. He clutched the .38 tighter.

The grass was loud under his feet. In his ears, blood rolled deep and loud.

Rudy opened the front door on the Capitan, and leaned limply on the knob. Neither spoke. When the silence had compressed into something almost hard and unbreakable, and both men had begun to gum words forward, a gun shot off. Both men flinched, frightened. Both of them also sighed, relieved at the shattered silence.

A few soldiers began to gather closer, coming from their posts leaned against trees, or sitting on lawn chairs.

"Mr. Sellers? Rudy?" the Capitan asked. He looked over both shoulders. "We ought to go right away."

Rudy tried not to let his eyes lay too long or familiar on the Capitan's face.

The Capitan announced theatrically, "Your family is under arrest."

Not too much later the Capitan watched Leticia lead Rudy to their seats in the back of the jeep, and in an attempt to placate the anxious soldiers nearby the Capitan waved them into the house.

"Take what's left," he barked. When they were all inside, the Capitan moved quickly across the yard.

"Oh, Capitan," a voice called from the front door.

It was the young soldier, the Capitan's assistant leaning a hip against the doorframe with one arm hung up from the transom, like he would no longer be bothered with any of the Capitan's orders even so much as to stand straight.

Tre fell headlong into his old backyard. He'd sprinted underneath the avocado tree and peeked into his parents' bedroom window knowing already that the sounds inside were sign enough that he was too late. He had to watch, some piece of him had to, as one soldier smoked a cigarette down to its butt and pressed the thing smoking onto Leticia's vanity mirror.

The mirror reflected the wide window into the backyard, the avocado tree out there, and what was crouched in its shade: Tre holding the .38 between two prayered hands.

The soldier's face brightened, a quality of light more than emotion.

"What is it?" The Capitan called to the young soldier in the doorway, not even bothering to turn. "I've got to go."

"To the plane?" the young soldier asked, his eyebrows rising. "Maybe I'll come along."

"The only place you're going is into that house." The Capitan glanced to Rudy and Leticia in the jeep. Neither met his eyes.

"Look," the young soldier said. He chuckled. He slapped the doorframe, giddy. "It's like magic. I go through this door and I'm this rank, with this job." He was pointing at his own chevrons. His new uniform had been altered poorly, cut too tight in the belly and too snug in the crotch like a baby's romper. "But when I come back out, I'll be that rank, with yours." He pointed at the bars on the Capitan's lapels.

"Swear it," the Capitan said. "You stay here."

"I'll swear that if you're retired now, too. Otherwise, things could get slippery."

The Capitan bit a scale of skin off his lip. "Thanks, soldier. But I came to that realization on my own."

The young soldier tossed a salute off the top of his brow, said, "You always were someone to emulate," and shut the door.

At this last comment, the Capitan hung his head. Those of us who believed he had changed felt he hung his head because he realized that the young soldier was right. Everyone had to learn from someone, and the Capitan had, regrettably, performed exceedingly well as a mentor in treachery.

Beside the doors of the old mission style church in Playas, the birds grew restless in their cages. Nora stood on the steps in her wedding dress, watching the wide street free of downtown traffic on a Sunday, waiting for the Capitan, and she had been telling the stodgy women with their military husbands damn the superstition if he saw her.

She didn't have a watch on her slim wrist to check. She only knew things were taking too long, or else the men and women in their over starched suits and uniforms and dresses wouldn't be so intent on getting her back inside.

She kept herself occupied by studying the birds caged in the flowerbeds at the entrance. Their glazed eyes were dark and depthless, giving back globed pieces of the bars and branches.

Tre had crept around to the front yard, where he hid on his belly in the overgrown bushes of a long-lost neighbor's abandoned house. Occasionally a soldier clopped by muttering into a walkietalkie. Tre was not a superstitious person, but he had to acknowledge that the Capitan's soldiers were taking too long to find him and, more importantly, he recognized the young soldier who had stopped to speak to the Capitan. In his experience, when you got so any powerful man could recognize you, or you him, no good could come of it. There was not much he could do, and he took the opportunity as soon as the jeep pulled away to leave cover of the bushes and chase after it. He even risked calling out, once, because the Capitan, whether he was trying to help or not, might as well have been on his way to the pier and to drive Tre's parents straight off its end.

Whatever sound Tre made trying to catch the jeep was enough to get the front door open one more time. The young soldier, expecting the Capitan, threw the door open wide and barked a laugh. "Magic," he said, slapping the doorframe. His smile fell when he saw Tre. He looked around for soldiers to call but, flustered and frightened, could only repeat his misfired taunt of the Capitan, "Magic."

Tre didn't even need to chop stride to shoot him. Some things, it's easy to forget how to do. Others you don't forget, even if you try.

The young soldier crumpled in the doorway, holding his thigh. He kept choking back sobs, and only managed to fight the tears by whipping himself into a red-faced frenzy. "Shoot him," he shouted, staring at the blood on his hand, the dark circle widening near his crotch. "Get me a jeep."

When the soldiers only stood over him, unmoved, he looked from each young face to the other. He collected himself with a breath through gritted teeth. "First shoot him," he instructed, calmly. "And then get me the jeep." When he saw that they all finally understood, were shaking their heads with him that there could be no more confusion, he burst: "Now. You goddam chicken fuckers."

Even at this speed, Tre's legs fetching him forward in leaps, he knew he'd never catch the jeep. He could shoot into the air, try to alert his parents, but that would only bring the soldiers down on him. He could shoot out a tire, but he wasn't ready to resort to that. He was hoping to use the jeep to get them all far from here fast. One thing occurred to him. The first shot with a gun was always the hardest, and his hadn't worked out too bad. What if he made things easy on himself? What if he just took out the Capitan?

His breathing came ragged, and dusty, and hot. Anyway, he couldn't line up the ridged nose of the barrel with the Capitan's head, at least not without occasionally eclipsing the heads of his mother or father. Only two people were missing from that car, and then the jeep might as well have been a goddam family wagon. He refused to lower the pistol, angry now, seeing that as lowering any last hope. He charged on, gaining.

The Capitan's head loomed large behind the sight.

And then the Capitan's head blurred into two, only now one was Nora's. The couple kissed, a soft one, and Nora threw her head back laughing so freely Tre thought she'd never stop, and he was young and in his family's home again, singing with his mother, wondering what about the books made Nora and his father laugh, or cry, and was it magic?

No. He couldn't kill the Capitan. That was his people now.

The shot didn't come from Tre's .38, but it took him too long to notice—though just an instant. The second shot he felt like a brick against his ribcage. He slid across the pavement a few feet, the soldiers frozen many yards away, and watching him, sure as Tre that this meant death. The Capitan's assistant slouched against the doorframe clutching his bloody thigh in one hand, and with the other, firing a pistol at the shrinking jeep, at the innocent people ducking out of and into the surrounding houses.

Tre thought he'd have gotten closer than this, the wheels of the jeep rolling far away, dizzying him. Suddenly the weight of death was whatever weight kept him down. He needed to stand, to run, and to die before he'd ever touched the ground, and somehow he felt that would not be death at all.

The wind sucked back into his lungs and he was up, barreling away from the small group of soldiers coming now out of the house, calling surprise to see him move. If Tre thought he owed his past life nothing, maybe he'd been wrong all along. Maybe things weren't so easy as becoming a new man, and he needed now more than ever for the old man to show. Tre thumbed the jacket where it was tattered by the bullet, but still hard, over his ribs. For once, he thought the Negra might not think the jacket so tacky. He couldn't forget the hard feeling of the earth, like a magnet, the enormous sky on his back, cold blue stone.

The jeep, by now, had sped off. Too far to catch. Tre'd be caught by bullets if he tried that straight-line chase.

He couldn't call it thought that tugged him through a narrow passage between two houses and down their alley toward the square. It wasn't fear that told him to duck, though he did that when the wall's stucco burst above his head, filling his eyes with dust. It wasn't any voice in his head, like they make it out in the movies or books, that told him what he had to do next. It was him. It was just him. He could have been better with words, but he knew instinct was the wrong word, too beastly. For this. This was the most human of passions—salvation.

He knew he'd only have one more chance to stop the jeep, when it came around the square to reach the freeway. And he knew the square was his only chance at life, his only chance at escape. Not just his, but his family's. Something he now felt profoundly. Like he'd shout it if he had the breath to. He'd been chased before. Been shot at. But never before had he really felt the flight. Never before had he been too concerned with dying. This time, though, he was hardly on this earth, the desire for escape tugged so hard at his being that it seemed to open spaces in him for the wind to pass. To escape. And to help his parents escape.

And to be back in the arms of the Negra.

Tre couldn't bear it any longer, and knew the square was coming. He remembered the tide of birds that had nearly overwhelmed him on his motorcycle, but in the end had saved him, taken him up into the air with them as far as his pursuers had known.

Now he was gasping for breath, and smiling too in relief. That relief had finally tugged so hard at him that he couldn't feel himself take the last cramped turn against the alley, couldn't feel the cobble stones come under his feet as he plowed out into the surrounding open square.

There. Across the sunlit cobbles—the cobbles were strange, and vast, and empty, but he didn't notice that—the jeep was crossing slowly and Tre finally had his shot. Maybe not the Capitan. No, he wouldn't do that. But a tire, if he needed to.

Tre slowed to take aim, confidence rising, striding now over the cobbles and their eerie echoes of his steps reaching out into spaces that shaped sound in ways that didn't belong, that weren't known, not to him, or to any of us from that place until now.

He cocked the hammer back. Too loud a clack. All there was in that empty square, really.

"No birds," Leticia said.

The Capitan touched the button to lock the doors of the vehicle, though the sun reminded him there was no roof, and the wind had already dried his eyes. He laughed then, a little, at himself. The job was finally almost done. Stiffly, he raised a hand up to his shoulder, a note between his fingers.

"From Nora?" Rudy was watching the Capitan's hazel eyes in the rear-view mirror—they'd flickered briefly at the name—and Rudy took the folded note.

"You'll be fine," the Capitan said. "I won't be able to wait with you. But I'll get you to where you need to wait and from there you might as well be free."

Leticia was watching something over a shoulder.

"What is it?" the Capitan asked.

"What's all the shooting? I saw some thug running from your men, back there."

"Who was it?" the Capitan asked.

She hefted her carriage against the stiff seat, and she sniffed proudly. "How should I know?" she asked, still looking back. "My husband was a professor, you know."

"Of course." The Capitan cleared his throat. "I wasn't thinking. About you being safe, maybe you wouldn't believe that if it was just from me to you, and I don't blame you. But, I promised your daughter. I gave her my word."

Rudy snorted and something rattled in his throat, turned into a cough that lasted a long time and hunched him over. The ride jostled his hunched figure side to side. When he sat up his long face was splotched red and the nostrils of his long-since broken nose were moist. Rudy handed Leticia the note for her to read it too.

Leticia rolled her eyes up to watch for something. "So you're finally making her an honest woman." Her hand found Rudy's, and his squeezed hers. Soon both of their knuckles went white, and Leticia exhaled a soft, "Oh." Rudy's hand patted Leticia's in apology.

"It's okay," Leticia said. She went back to watching out the window, this time wondering: when they'd driven past the square, why hadn't there been a single bird in the sky? Under her breath, she said, "Not a single one."

Nothing in the square fought sound. The tall thin buildings stared dark-draped windows at one another, like even they refused to look at Tre. The sky was clear of clouds, of sun, of anything at all.

Birds pocked the cobbles like discarded rags.

What wings remained open were balding where you'd expect finer feathers, and bright.

A soldier stood alone in the square, watching Tre slow to a clumsy walk.

The soldier, puzzled, returned to scraping a steel shovel across the cobbles, bird carcasses rolling before it, and he cursed the shovel anytime it caught the cobblestones. The shovel-blade rose, scraped on again.

The jeep rolled out of sight, and combat boots hammered sound into something cold and hard and flat. Escape was already reshaping itself in Tre's mind. No longer a tugging outward, now a pulling inward; a steady fall and then the feeling of landing into oneself. So long as it wasn't the ground. The ground was death, and the body was the weight that held us to it. Still the shovel scraped along, rolling the small feathered bodies forward. Some of their feathers fell away, floated off, but not too many.

Tre turned from the road now empty of the jeep. He faced the expected soldiers, lined up neatly. He faced down so many rifle barrels' round black eyes.

Many years later, as he faced the firing squad... Tre must have thought, grinning.

He planted his feet and, just as the scraping shovel ceased, he raised the .38.

After the shots, again, it was silent.

He fell hard, but onto small soft things.

The huge metal hanger door scraped open. A bright day chased the dark further inside. Then the young soldier lurched into the doorway and seemed to call that dark back to form his shadow, one arm upraised. The other arm he used to keep his long coat wrapped tightly.

Rudy and Leticia hadn't been waiting in the dark room of the warehouse for too long, but they were already exhausted, their nerves smoldering, their stomachs on fire from shrinking, slouched over each other but too jittery to sit. They had the clothes on their backs, and not much else. Rudy had a few books weighing down his pockets. They each had a milk jug filled with water and strung through the handle was a rope so they'd hang from shoulders like gourds.

Rudy stepped forward, though not far, and he raised a hand to the light. There was no reason to lie. If they were caught, they were caught. He understood that better than he'd understood anything ever. He nodded.

The young soldier nodded, too, and when the light traveled up and down his cheekbones Rudy thought he looked pale, but familiar.

"Come on then," the young soldier said.

"Can we speak to the Capitan again?"

"In a way," he said. "You knew he couldn't be here. He must have told you that when you all arranged this. Right?"

Rudy shrugged. "You're right."

"Say it again." The young soldier rested a shoulder against the door. Breathing was a chore, but he managed force when he said, "Say it louder."

"You're right," Rudy said.

The young soldier smiled. "Thanks."

He walked them slowly but boldly across the tarmac, and they both clutched their water jugs closely to their chests. Their heads were dropped like that would hide them.

"In there," the young soldier said, tugging the arms of his coat off. The sun forced his eyes nearly shut.

The rear of the plane gaped dark and wide in front of them. When Rudy looked back the young soldier was smoking, was wearing like a cloak the coat that had been hiding the bloody bullet wound in his thigh.

The plane's rotors spun into round blurs. The plane taxied on the tarmac and sat for a while.

The ramp was rising, closing, and at the last moment Rudy saw the young soldier remove a recording device from a blood-darkened pocket in his trousers. It was a sleek black device that hardly filled the young soldier's bloody palm. Say it louder… Rudy remembered. He understood now that he had given away the Capitan, given away Nora.

The young soldier had to wipe the device clean of blood many, many times. He pressed a button proudly and held the device with a shaking hand against his ear. It made no sound. Or was it just that Rudy couldn't hear over the plane's engines? As if by habit, the young soldier searched for the tape in the recorder, but there didn't seem to be any place for one. He smacked the sleek recording device once, twice, and listened again to nothing before letting the recorder clatter at his feet. Both of his ears were red with blood by the time the rising door wiped him and the world out of the picture.

The church doors burst open.

The bride and groom rushed out, the birds rushed the sky, and the groom rushed to watch the street for military jeeps and soldiers. He couldn't see a thing but flapping wings. He had to fight not to swat at them. He lifted a hand, but saw in Nora's eyes the same kind of frantic searching that must have filled his own. If they hadn't come after him by now, perhaps they would not come at all. He took her hand then.

She smiled and shook her head in agreement with something.

The birds were gone and the couple hardly noticed, kissing, as they were, the clapping of the audience overpowering any flapping of wings.

It was black. Musty in the plane's belly. The walls were hot from the sun outside. But the black was shifting, alive, and Rudy called out. Only Leticia answered, saying she was here, nearby. Rudy took a match from a small sliding box in his chest-pocket and scraped it once, twice before a light flared.

Retreating faces. Rudy gasped, the match snuffed, and the smoke burned in his sinuses. "Who's here?"

Someone gripped his arms. Leticia on one side. God knows who on the other. "What are we doing here?" Rudy asked the people he now sensed on all sides of them.

Shuffling sounds. Hard bare feet, fine hard heels.

A man said, "That ain't a real question, is it?"

Rudy made to light another match but didn't, nodding solemnly.

The people must have clustered, even in the dark, to the back of the cargo hold. They must have clawed for grips on the bare black walls. When the cargo hold's door gaped open, the sky that day, that they saw from within, that we all saw from somewhere, was bright and blue as flame. There were no clouds. When the plane rose higher and higher until its belly's floor was only a dim slope down which to slide, the orange horizon rose sharply out of sight like a curtain. All was a wide flat stage of blue water, like diamonds hammered by a precise hand, polished, blinding. And on through the rushing wind they went, two by two, down to the shining sea.

Fifty-Three

An old woman with a hunched back, curled grey hair, and rain boots folded like a colonialist's though the day was sunny, counted them flying one by one into their cage beneath the grape arbor. She squinted a monocled eye over her ticking pointer finger.

The beaming newlyweds watched, Nora seated at the table, her Capitan standing behind. When the old woman muttered to herself and began her count again, Nora bit her thumbnail and said, "Oh I hope none are missing."

A clapping came from somewhere above, and the old woman said, "Here they come. Don't you worry, Dear."

"My husband and I have a bet," Nora said. "Are all of these ours?"

The old woman shrugged her shoulders. "Others' too."

"What did I tell you?" the Capitan said, and kissed Nora's cheek. He drank greedily from the glass of wine at the table, and studied the tiny coils of vine above his head. "One day, we'll drink our own. Just me and you."

Nora ducked closer to the cage, one light hand trailing back to hook a finger into the Capitan's belt. She pressed her pretty face close to the cage, a light wind lifting the hair above her forehead. Pulling the Capitan closer, she said, "Look. Look."

She looked to her Capitan, her eyes begging him to understand the meaning. Could he tell she'd resigned herself to feeling a way about something?

She sensed him tugging away, returning to his wine glass out of his fear of misinterpreting her meaning and disappointing her. She released him, and stroked the back of his arm instead. He set the glass back down, without having taken the drink he meant to.

"One instant," she explained to him, fluttering her hands, "they're like ghosts up there." She wanted for the two of them to lift their looks together past her hands, to the sky. "And the next..." They had never quite looked past one another. She said it barely, sweetly, moving in to kiss him: "The next instant, this little feathered thing's perched quiet in your face." What she meant was that their journey was over. Not just the birds'. What she meant was that she had arrived, finally. Nora was a woman of a higher station. "All of this," she said. "I have only you to thank for all of this."

He was silent for a long while. "I see that now," her Capitan confessed.

Fifty-Four

From high above the Clearwater barrios, the square at their center gaped wide and cracked and dry. The dark cobblestones catching the sun were living scales, and they tugged two small figures across the square, into the shade of the fountain. The boy's smooth feet wore dust from the roads, stark as bones on the cobbles. The Negra's feet were darker than the stones she stood on.

Cigarette butts rounded the fountain making the Negra think of dried petals and she cursed that she hadn't brought no flowers. In the tub of the empty fountain was a bird's foot. The boy spotted it, and he leaned in, picked the forked thing up, and thumbed its dried ridges. He thought he'd made sure the Negra didn't see him when he stuck it into his pocket for good luck.

Because she was a mother now, and because she knew boys, she let him keep it. He was old enough for dead things, but also not too old yet for luck. And he was also old enough that he wouldn't sit beside her, even though she asked.

She kept on speaking things to him. We were all very happy she did that for the boy. No one ever gossiped or spoke ill of her anymore. We knew by then that it was never too early to begin a child's education. Hopping, dancing, dusty face painted wet-yellow with sun. His shadow leaped full-grown beside him, its ghost-head thrown back on the cobblestones, the boy's head thrown back on the sky, laughing.

It wouldn't matter if the boy listened to her that day—she knew that, and we all did, too. One day he'd hear the story in his head like it was his own voice, or all voices, or like those two were the same thing.

She just sat at the fountain and let the boy play, let the boy dance, and laughed with him.

Watching the two of them, tiny and far off shadows in that square alone, you couldn't hear her say one word. But we knew better. We knew it since that story about the baby's death—murder, really. We knew that this is how you tell a story, if you want anyone to listen. You whisper.

The end.

Acknowledgements

The author gratefully acknowledges the editors of the journals in which his stories and novel excerpts first appeared. Special thanks is also due to the following: Gail & Louis Rosales, Alexandria Rosales, Ramon Rosales, Bryan Gonzalez, Lindsey Clemons, and Stephen Graham Jones.

CPSIA information can be obtained
at www.ICGtesting.com
Printed in the USA
FFOW03n0359170517
35655FF